FOCUSED

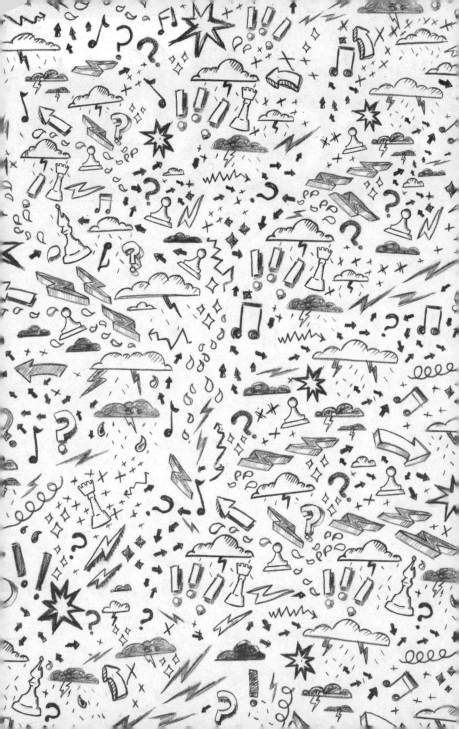

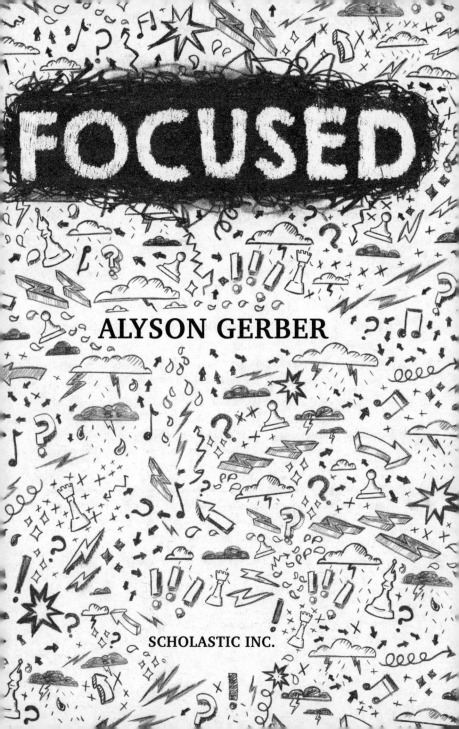

FOCUSED

ALYSON GERBER

SCHOLASTIC INC.

ISBN 978-1-338-53167-1

10 9 8 7 6 5   20 21 22 23

Printed in the U.S.A.   40

First printing 2019

Book design by Baily Crawford

For Andrew

I HAVE FORTY-FIVE minutes to finish five word problems, shower, get ready for school, and eat. I should have done all my homework last night, like probably everyone else in my class did. But the word problems this year are a lot harder than the ones we had to do last year, and I guess I thought that when I woke up this morning, the questions would be easier and less like blobs of letters that make zero sense. I was wrong. They're still impossible. And even though I'm the worst at math, I know that if I hand in five out of ten answers, my best-case grade is a *50*.

In other words, an F.

I can't let that happen.

My phone is buzzing. I'm pretty sure it's Red since he's the only one who ever texts me. I scan the room—bed, dresser, side table, floor. It's not here. Unless it's under the pile of clean clothes Mom asked me to fold and put away yesterday. But that doesn't even make sense. My phone is my alarm, so I had it a few minutes ago when it woke me up. It must have fallen off the table. I hang off the side of the bed and look. Phew. I pick it up, flip it over, and put it down next to me. I don't read the text. I can't let Red's message distract me from my homework. He'll totally get it when I tell him what happened. I mean, we're best friends, so he knows how my life will be ruined if I fail.

I sit up and read the first word problem: *Three friends— Jane, Jon, and Joe—are dividing up the proceeds from their local lemonade stand . . .* My stomach grumbles. I'm pretty hungry. Maybe I should shower, eat, and *then* do my homework. A toasted English muffin with melty peanut butter on one side and Nutella on the other might help me concentrate. Plus, it will only take me fifteen minutes, and then I'll still have thirty to finish math. Done. Great plan.

I shower as fast as I can, cover up my new forehead zit, gloss my lips, and throw on a light blue dress, because even though it makes me look like I'm trying too hard, a dress is an insta-outfit, and the clock is ticking. I don't have time to coordinate tops and bottoms right now. I need to make breakfast and get back to work.

I grab my textbook and run out of my bedroom and down the hall three minutes earlier than I'd planned. Winning! I'm rushing down the stairs and flipping back to the page about Jane, Jon, and Joe so I can read while I toast when my foot slides and slips out from under me. I grab for the railing, but I miss and fall backward, landing on the stairs.

What is wrong with me?

"Clea? Are you okay?" Mom asks, rushing over.

"I don't know." My voice sounds small and far away.

Mom helps me up, and once I'm standing, everything in my body feels weird and shocked and stiff. She bends down to pick up my textbook, wraps her arm around me, and leads me into the kitchen.

We sit down at the table, and she looks at me like she's really worried. "I know we've talked about this before, but you need to slow down and take your time, sweetheart. If you try to do everything at once, you're going to end up getting really hurt."

I want to scream, because I already know falling and not finishing my homework is my fault and none of this would have happened if I weren't so stupid and forgetful. But I don't want Mom to know about the word problems, so I nod and let her rub my back for a little longer.

Henley walks into the room, puts a granola bar on the table in front of me, and grabs on to my arm. She's in the same purple overalls she's been wearing every day for two weeks, ever since she turned six and a half and decided she was old enough to be in charge of picking her own outfits.

"You scared me," she says. Only she can't actually say the word *scared*, so it comes out sounding like *sca-wed*.

"I'm okay," I assure her. "Promise."

She looks up at me with her big blue eyes, checking to be sure I'm telling the truth.

I smile at her, unwrap the granola bar, and take a bite, because even though I know being hungry isn't the reason I fell, I don't want my sister to think about me for another second when she already has so many other things to worry about, like speaking up in school and enunciating her words and all the things that are hard for her.

If I can help it, at least one of us is going to have a good day.

When I get to school, Red is waiting at our bench. As soon as I see him, I remember—my phone. It's still in my room, and I never checked his message. *UGH. Stupid.*

He starts talking before I even get there. "So, are we not best friends anymore? Because I'm pretty sure even sort-of friends don't straight up ignore each other's texts."

"I'm sorry. We're definitely BFFs," I say. "I'm the worst."

"I needed you to answer." He sounds annoyed.

"I won't do it again." I look at him when I say it, because I want him to know I'm serious. "I was trying to finish my math homework, which I didn't even do, and then I forgot my phone in my room. I'll write back next time. I promise."

"Okay." He nods. "Thanks."

"What did you say in the text?" I ask.

"That I hate my dad, and now we have to talk every other day, because the lawyer says he deserves more 'quality time.' Maybe he should have thought of that before he moved across the country."

"That's not okay," I say.

"Yeah, not really." He looks down at his sneakers.

I wish there were something I could say to make it better, but I can't think of anything that will actually help.

"What are you going to do about math?" he asks.

I shake my head. "No clue. I mean, I have it first period. Suggestions welcome."

"Mmm, don't save your homework for the morning."
He grins.

"Because that's really helpful right now."

"You'll figure it out," he says. "You always do."

He has no idea how wrong he is.

I look around Ms. Pumi's room for the folded piece of paper that says CLEA ADAMS. She moves the name tags every single class so we can always learn from a "new perspective." I'd rather just sit in the same place.

I spot my name and walk over to my assigned seat for the day, which is at the far corner of the room next to Dylan.

Lucky me. Not.

He grunts a little when I sit down, like I'm bothering him, when he's the one who smells like ocean waves or some other gross boy-scented body mist that's making it hard for me to think about anything else.

I should take out my notebook, but I don't want to look at my half-finished worksheet now or ever. I still don't have a plan, and I'm starting to get scared. I can't get a bad grade on anything or I won't be allowed on the chess team. Chess is a special elective at our school, which means we practice during the day twice a week, and after school once a week. If your grades aren't good enough, you have to go to extra study hall instead. I need to make sure that doesn't happen, since chess is my number one favorite thing in the entire world. Maybe Ms. Pumi will be so excited about teaching fractions that she'll magically forget to collect our homework. Then it will be like this whole horrible blip of a morning never happened.

Ms. Pumi claps. "I'd like to start out by reviewing the homework from last night as a class. We'll go through each of the ten problems together. Could I have volunteers to show their work on the board?"

I raise my hand. This is my chance to (A) participate and (B) prove that I did the homework. I just need to be one of the first five people picked, because I don't have answers for the second half of the questions.

Ms. Pumi scans the room, looking at all the hands. "Jason—one."

I reach up even higher and sort of wave my fingers around in the air a little, in case she didn't see me before, but her eyes pass right by me. "Anna—two." *Ugh. Don't freak out. It's not over yet. There are still three more chances.* I stretch my arm up as high as it will go, and look right at Ms. Pumi, because eye contact usually works in these situations. She glances back at me, and I'm pretty sure she's about to say my name. I hold my breath and cross my fingers. *Please.*

"Dylan, why don't you answer number three?" *No. No. No. Dylan really doesn't need another chance to show off. He's already such a bragger. We all get it—math is so easy for him.* "Angela, go ahead and start on number four. And—" She pauses.

Please. Pick me. Please. Please—

"Pick me!" I blurt before I can stop the words from falling out of my mouth.

What's wrong with me?

"You need to wait until you're called on," Ms. Pumi chides.

I hear someone giggle.

I put my hand down and sink into my chair.

Ms. Pumi calls on a few other students, but I'm not listening. I keep my eyes glued to the floor and replay what I just did over in my mind, until I hear, "Clea—why don't you come on up and show us the answer to the last problem?"

I look up at her and shake my head.

"I'd like you to solve number ten," Ms. Pumi says, and I can tell by her tone that she's not asking this time. Everyone is staring again. Their eyes are burning into me, like they're all waiting for me to get up and figure it out already, instead of sitting here like a dummy.

I pick up my textbook and walk over to the board. I need to figure this out fast. *Joanna enters a baking contest in her town and wins a $350 grand prize. If she spent $20.35 on ingredients, $9.27 on equipment, and $3.29 on marketing materials, what percentage profit did she make on her big win?* I'm pretty sure I need to add, subtract, and then divide. But maybe that's wrong. I don't even know, and I'm running out of time.

"Is everything okay?" Ms. Pumi asks.

"Yes," I squeak. *Stop messing up. Just focus. Pull it together. She can't know you didn't do the homework.* I start writing the numbers on the board, because I definitely can't add them up in my head. Mental math is impossible for me. I don't get how people can do it. I can barely remember the numbers I'm writing down. I have to keep looking back at the book so I don't get them all wrong. I add five, seven, and nine and then carry the two, when Ms. Pumi says, "That's enough. Can someone who did the homework please come up to the board?"

I can't breathe. There's not enough air in the room.

"Ooh," someone says.

Everyone laughs.

"Don't do that." Ms. Pumi shoots them down, but it

9

doesn't change the fact that they all know there's something wrong with me. And now I'm definitely getting an F on the homework.

No matter what I do, chess is going to get taken away.

By the time I get to Spanish, almost every seat is taken. We're allowed to sit wherever we want, which is one of the many reasons Spanish is my favorite subject. But today picking our own seats doesn't seem so great, because even though I can tell that it's a front-row-by-the-window kind of day, the only open desk is smack in the middle of the room.

As soon as I slide into the chair, I feel cramped.

"¡Buenos días, estudiantes!" Señora Campo says, making her grand entrance in a black-and-white-striped skirt and bright red sweater. I love when she talks to us *en español*, like she knows we can handle it. It makes me feel like I can, and also like I'm being transported to Madrid, where word problems don't matter and my back and butt aren't sore from my fall. "I want to get a sense of all the wonderful things you remember from our lessons. So we are going to spend this period taking a pop quiz. I'd like you to think of this as an opportunity for us to check in and see where you are and where you need to be." She looks around the room and smiles at each of us. "Please take one and pass it on."

Before I even have a quiz, everyone around me is churning out answers and making me nervous. Lily hands me the stack of papers. I put one on my desk and turn to pass the rest of the pile on, but somehow everyone behind me has already started working, so I give the quizzes to Hunter, who's sitting next to me. Then I write my name and read the first question: *You are on vacation with your family and decide to rent bicycles to explore the sights*—the staple in the top corner is breaking apart, barely able to hold the pages together, because there are so many of them. I flip to the end and look at the number—10. *UGH*. This isn't a pop quiz—it's totally a pop *test*!

I glance at the clock. Only thirty minutes left, and I haven't done anything. I need to focus. *Write three sentences describing your bike ride through the city.*

What city? Any city? Did I miss that in the directions? I read them again, but it just says *vacation*. I don't have time to go up and ask Señora Campo. Plus, I don't want her to know I haven't even started.

My stomach grumbles. I really hope there's pizza at lunch. Hunter is chewing on his eraser and breathing hard, like he's running a marathon. And I guess this is kind of like the marathon of pop quizzes, but still. He needs to stop. It's impossible for me to think about anything else. It also doesn't help that I can't remember the Spanish word for *bicycle*. I should move on to the next question. This is such a waste of time. There are pencils everywhere, and they're so loud.

Lily is shaking out her hand, like it's tired from all the writing she's been doing, while I've been sitting here doing—I don't even know what. Nothing! I can't fail a quiz in my best subject. Bicicleta. *Duh!*

The bell rings. Everyone gets up, except for me. I don't want Señora Campo to think that the only thing I remember in Spanish is my name.

The whole class clears out of the room. I make a move to go, but I guess I lose track of my own leaving, because Señora Campo walks over and sits down next to me. I'm going to be late for chess. "Is everything okay, Clea?" she asks.

I don't know. I mean, it's not, and I want to tell her, but I have no idea what to say or where to start. Hunter is a heavy breather. People need to turn down the volume on their pencils. My brain got stuck on question one. I sat here being mad at myself. It's like out of nowhere the time disappeared on me. And I'm not sure where it went.

Señora Campo picks up my test and flips through the first few pages. They're all blank. "I know you sometimes need a few extra minutes to finish up, but—" She stops herself and sighs—the loud kind that echoes off the walls and back at me. It's the worst sound I've ever heard, because now I know for sure that she's disappointed. I don't know what to say or do to go back to when she thought I was smart and good at Spanish and could handle anything. It stings behind my eyes.

"I know the answers," I tell her. "Really. I do." Because even though I didn't actually have a chance to read all the questions, I still think that could be true. And now I'm worried about my grade and chess and all the things I'm going to lose if this is really happening.

She nods. "I'm sure you do. I don't want you to be too late for next period."

"But what about the quiz?" I ask.

"We'll see," she says.

I know that's really not good.

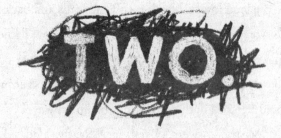

THE HALLWAY IS empty. It's quiet, except for muffled teacher voices, reminding me that next period has already started and I'm late for chess when I can't be. Today is the first game of the year and my chance to prove I'm ready to be one of the twelve people who gets picked to play in tournaments and help our team win the championship. I sprint across the hall, down the stairs, and over to the multipurpose room. *How could I let this happen? I'm such an idiot. I can't do anything right.* I should have asked Señora Campo if we could talk about the quiz at recess or lunch or any time other than during chess. Or, better yet, I could have just not messed up.

All I needed to do was finish the questions, like everyone else in my entire class who isn't an idiot.

By the time I get to chess, I feel like I might puke. I think about turning around and going to the nurse and giving up on this stupid day. I wouldn't even have to lie about being sick to my stomach, because I am.

Even though I'm scared of getting in trouble for being dumb and late, I know playing chess is the only thing that will make me feel better right now. I take a deep breath, push open the creaky door, and walk into the room as quietly as I can, trying not to draw attention to myself. I can feel everyone's eyes on me as I look around for my place at the long tables lined with chessboards and clocks. Every seat is taken, except for the one across from Sanam—the best player on our team. That's not official or anything, but it's obvious that Sanam and Red are better than everyone else.

Great. Just, great. I'm in trouble.

Sanam doesn't glance up at me when I sit down. Her big brown eyes stay glued to the pieces, like she isn't going to let anything get in her way of winning. She looks like a chess queen perched in front of the board, wearing a denim shirt and tiny gold studs. It's impossible to tell how small and slight she really is.

Layla is sitting next to me, biting her fingernails and making loud slurping noises. She needs to stop chewing so I can pay attention to Mr. Lee. I keep waiting for Sanam to say something to Layla, but Sanam's still staring at the board between us, like she's too busy thinking through her opening to notice, which is another thing I should be doing. There is a pink hair elastic strangling my wrist. I take it off, spin it around my fingers, and look at the pieces in front of me. I need a strong start if I'm going to win. Only I can't think about anything other than the human garbage disposal sitting next to me.

"Can you stop biting your nails?" I mutter.

Layla glares at me. "What's your problem?"

"Nothing," I whisper. "You're just so loud."

She rolls her eyes.

"Everyone needs to be listening to what I'm saying right now. Not talking. Is that clear?" Mr. Lee looks at me.

I nod and swallow hard.

Everyone is staring at me, like they know I have a defect that makes it impossible for me not to mess up.

Mr. Lee tucks his hands into his pockets and walks across the room. "We all want to win the championship this year, and your performance in practice is a big part of how I'll decide who will be competing. We have five regular season tournaments starting next Saturday. I expect all of you to be present and prepared to play."

"*And* you have to actually show up on time, *Clea*," Dylan says under his breath, but loud enough so everyone around us can hear. He leans back in his chair, pushing the front legs off the ground.

My face and neck feel hot, and I'm pretty sure I'm turning red, but I don't say anything back to him, because I don't want him to ask why I was late. I need to forget about the quiz so I can play my best and win.

"Any questions before we start?" Mr. Lee asks.

No hands go up.

"Okay. Get to work," he says to everyone, and then he walks over to me. "Let's chat for a minute."

I stand up and follow him away from the tables. My heart is beating hard inside my chest. I read the secret T-shirt he's wearing under his thin plaid button-down—*Death Cab for Cutie*. I think it's a band that's really good. All of the T-shirts he wears have music or plays or books on them. They're kind of hard to see hidden under his teacher clothes, but I usually find a way. I think it's the second coolest part about him. The coolest part is that he's a National Master, which is a really high ranking in chess. Our matches aren't officially rated, because our middle school is in a league with other private schools where that isn't allowed, so I don't know where I stand exactly, but I'm aiming to be a National Master in high school.

"I'm sorry I was late," I say before Mr. Lee has a chance to point it out first. "I—it won't happen again. I swear." I don't want him to think I'm full of excuses or bad at school and horrible at following rules, even though I really am. I had a tutor this summer—Chloe-Louise. She tried to help me with reading comprehension and being organized, but it obviously didn't make a difference, because I'm still the same.

"Clea, I want you to understand why you need to be on time for chess," Mr. Lee says. "If I've selected you to play in a tournament and you're late for the first round, you might be forced to forfeit the game, and every point counts. Or I could decide to replace you with one of our alternates. Being picked to represent our team is an honor for top players, who have shown they're serious about chess. I need to be able to trust that you're going to be here or I won't be able to pick you to compete. Does that make sense?"

I nod. "You can count on me," I say, because I want that to be true more than anything.

"I'm glad to hear it," he says and smiles, like he understands that it was a mistake and it's okay this one time, as long as it never happens again.

When I sit back down, I hit the clock. Sanam is playing white, which means she has the first move, but I get to start the game. And I'm ready. I don't need more time. I want to play chess so I can stop thinking about everything else.

Sanam slides the pawn in front of her king up two squares. She taps the clock and writes down the first move in her scorebook.

It's a trap. A classic Sicilian setup. I memorized the top ten chess traps of all time so I'd be able to use them in tournaments, but I never thought about what would happen if someone tried to corner me. Now my time is ticking away, and I'm not sure what to do. I don't mirror Sanam's move, because that feels really right, and traps play on instincts, which means it can't be a good decision. Instead I move my pawn on the queen's side up two squares, tap the clock, and write down what I did. *Move. Let go. Tap. Write.* I hum the words in my head as a way to sing them into my memory. I need to remember all the steps if I'm going to win. Mr. Lee treats every match like a tournament, where we're disqualified if we don't

keep a record of the game. He wants everything about playing chess to be second nature.

Sanam's forehead folds up. I'm pretty sure she was expecting something else from me, because she doesn't do anything
for almost a minute. It's weird to watch her stall. She clears her
throat, taps her perfectly painted yellow fingernails on the table,
and glances at the clock. She takes a deep breath and develops
her knight—up two squares and over one—*clop, clop, clop.*

I move my pawn.

Sanam moves her pawn.

Once I get into the rhythm, all I see are answers everywhere. There are patterns on the board that make it clear
where each piece is supposed to go next, like a bunch of connected mazes that all lead to one place—the enemy king. My
heart beats faster. I can't stop tapping my toes. I'm stuck in a
word-proof, sound-proof, everything-proof tunnel.

All that matters are the pieces in front of me.

I started playing chess last year. It was Red's idea. He
thought I'd be a natural. We've never been in the same class,
except for homeroom, which doesn't count, because there are
no grades or assignments or homework. I've told him about
all the problems I had in school last year, and he still thinks

I'm smart like he is. I want to argue with him about that, but he won't let me.

The reason I said yes to joining the chess team in the first place was that last year was hard-slash-bad for Red. His parents got divorced and his dad moved to a fancy, faraway ski town in Colorado with his girlfriend, Barb (aka Barf), and I wanted to be a good friend.

At first, I thought chess would be boring and way too hard for me, like math. But once I started playing, I realized it was actually fun. It's sort of like a video game and a puzzle and tennis all put together, except so much better.

My next move against Sanam is obvious—take her pawn out with my pawn—and for a second it seems too good to be true. I stop myself and think through all the possibilities to make sure I'm not being trapped into something that might appear like an awesome idea now, but isn't. Once I've played through the next few steps in my mind and I'm confident, I let go of my piece.

Sanam uses her knight to take out my pawn. Good. I was counting on that.

I move my knight and tap the clock.

When I look up, Sanam is placing her knight down.

I move my other knight out, because I think I can win this way—I know I can.

A few people on the team are whispering behind me, but I don't look up. I'm too busy thinking about the board and Sanam and making the right next move.

Sanam captures another one of my pieces and taps the clock without realizing that she's left my rook on an empty file with direct access to her king. I slide my rook in a straight line across the board. *Checkmate! I did it! I won!*

"Wooo-hoooo!" Red shouts.

I look up and he's standing there grinning at me.

There are fireworks going off in my brain—green and red and blue and yellow.

I reach out to shake Sanam's hand. "Good game." My words sound happy, like they're bouncing off a trampoline and flying around in the air.

She shakes my hand back, but doesn't say anything. She gives her score sheet to Mr. Lee as fast as she can, like she can't wait to get rid of it.

"You dominated that game," Red says.

"You should have seen Sanam's opening. I dodged a serious trap."

He puts up his hand, and I high-five him.

"Nice job, Clea." Mr. Lee pats my back. "I can tell you've put in a lot of time. It's paying off. Keep up the hard work."

I can't stop smiling, because I won and Mr. Lee noticed that I'm even better than before. For a few minutes, I'm floating on a cloud of victory, until I remember everything else that happened today.

After school, I sit outside on the curb by the main pickup area and wait for Mom. There are no other students left. It's just me. Some of the teachers are even starting to leave. Mom was supposed to be here thirty minutes ago, which means I should be doing my homework right now. Even though I'm the one who made up the rule that I have to get started by 4:00 p.m., it still feels like I'm behind. And after today, I need to find a way to make sure that never happens again.

I drop my bag and start pacing, until Mom finally pulls up at 4:05 p.m. "Sorry I'm so late," she says when I open the car door.

"I'm *saw-weee*, too," Henley squeaks from the backseat. "Ms. B had a special surprise for Mommy!"

"Really?" I turn around to face her. "What was it?" Her dirty-blond hair is sticking out in every direction and her cheeks are red and splotchy, like she's been running around outside on a snowy day. Henley is all dimples and soft, sweet features. I'm hard lines and lots of reddish-brown hair.

"Chocolate gummy bears!" Henley smiles with her whole face. "I saved one." She holds out a mushy, chocolate-covered hand.

"Thank you." I smile and pop her present into my mouth.

She looks out the window and lets her legs swing side to side. "I love speech," she says softly to no one in particular. It's more like a quiet announcement. Henley is my favorite person on earth. She makes me almost forget I'm mad at Mom for being late.

Henley has a hard time hearing and speaking up and pronouncing words. It sounds like some of her letters get caught in a warm, sticky pot of caramel. They're gooey and garbled and coated in sweetness. Her speech therapist, Ms. B (for Blumenthal), told Mom that she has to practice using her own voice more. She said I make that hard. I guess it's because Henley doesn't have to say very much to me. She can point and make a face, and I pretty much always know exactly what she wants. I didn't realize the whole special sister mind-reading thing was hurting her or I never would have done it in the first place.

"Henley, as soon as we get home, you're going straight into the tub," Mom says.

"NO! No bath!" she shouts. "I want to play with Clea!"

"I have to do homework, but we can play chess or whatever else you want this weekend," I say. "Promise."

"Chess! Teach me!" she says, forgetting about her bath. "Can you, me, and Hilda play *togefer*?"

"Duh!" I say. "We'd never leave Hilda out." It doesn't matter that Hilda is our dog, and can't play chess. Henley doesn't like to exclude anyone.

"Duh!" Henley imitates me.

"Thank you," Mom mouths to me.

I shrug. I don't like it when she thanks me for being nice to my sister, like it's a chore, when it's not.

Once we get home, I go straight upstairs to my room and turn on the thunderstorm soundtrack Chloe-Louise gave me. It's supposed to make homework easier. So far, all it does is make me feel like it's raining. But apparently I need to "be patient" and "give it a chance," because any minute now it's going to start helping.

Hilda scurries into my room and jumps onto my bed, digging and circling three times before she finally gives in and folds herself into a tiny black fluff ball. That's been her thing for the last three months, ever since Mom let me visit the rescue dogs at the MSPCA. I wanted to adopt every single dog in the entire place, because I love animals, but Mom flat-out rejected that idea, and said I had to pick one. As soon as I saw Hilda, I knew she belonged in our family.

My first choice to rename Hilda was Pumpernickel, because her fur reminds me of pumpernickel bread, which is my favorite, even if Red thinks it's disgusting. But I felt like coming into a new home with a new family would be a lot of change at once, and Hilda might want to keep her old name, since it was all that was left from her past.

Homework. I have to do homework. Although first I have to put on more comfortable clothes.

Then I sit down on the floor and look through my planner, because starting right now, I'm going to be super organized and prepared and on top of everything. I take out Spanish and math. I need to finish both assignments before dinner, and then, after I eat, I'll do history and science and practice my author presentation for Mr. Lee's English class until it's perfect.

My phone is buzzing somewhere. It's not next to me or in my pocket. I check my backpack, and then I stand up and look all around my room, but I can't find it. *UGH. Seriously? Where did I leave it this time?* I know it's probably Red calling me, and I can't flake out on him again. I promised I wouldn't, so I need to find my phone now, before he stops believing me. I open my closet. The dress I wore all day is on the floor. I kick it away, but my phone isn't there. That's when I remember—I didn't have it at school. It's still on my bed where I left it this morning! I grab it and call Red back.

"I hate waiting for my dad to call," Red says as soon as he picks up. "He's always late. And I don't need to be reminded that he doesn't care about me. He moved to Colorado, so that's pretty clear."

"I'm sorry," I say.

"The worst part is that I was actually excited to tell him about chess. And now I'm just mad that he's late."

I sit back down on the floor next to my backpack. "That really stinks."

"Yeah, it does. Can you stay on the phone until he calls?"

"Of course," I say, because I'm glad there's something I can do to help.

"It might be kind of a while. Last time, I waited forty-eight minutes."

"I'm not hanging up," I say.

"Thanks." He takes a deep breath like he's relieved.

It's already 5:06 p.m. I glance down at the blank worksheet in front of me. "But I need to do homework while we wait. I have kind of a lot."

"Me too," he says. "There's so much more this year."

"You think so, too? I thought it was just me."

"No way. Seventh grade is a lot harder."

It feels good to hear him say that, like we're the same. And maybe if I work hard from now on, I can fix my grades and still play chess. I put my phone on speaker so I don't have to hold it up to my ear while I start Spanish.

"Clea, why is it raining in your room?" he asks.

"Oh. I forgot that was on," I say. "It's supposed to help me concentrate or whatever."

"Does it?"

"Um, yeah," I say, because that's what I want the answer to be.

"Cool."

I open my textbook. *Imagine you can see into the future of a famous person you admire . . .* I point to each word and try to block out the sound of Red breathing into the phone. *Write at least five sentences in Spanish explaining what will happen to this person tomorrow morning, afternoon, and night.* I make it to the end of the directions, but I'm not sure what I'm supposed to do. The words don't sink in. They fall away and disappear like raindrops off a thick plastic coat.

I close my eyes and try to let the stormy sounds help me focus. I need to finish *something* before dinner. Only, Red is still breathing loudly, and Mom is rummaging around in the kitchen, banging pots and pans together and talking to herself or Henley or someone on the phone. I want to turn off all the noises, because it's almost time to eat and I haven't done anything!

"He's calling," Red says. "I want it to be normal, like before."

"Maybe act like it is, and it will be."

"Okay. I mean, it can't hurt," he says. "Thanks for being the same."

"No problem," I say, even though right now I really wish I could be different.

"Clea!" Mom shouts.

I put my pencil down on the blank piece of paper in front of me, shut off the thunderstorm, and walk out of my room.

Downstairs it smells like butter and sautéed vegetables, and I know right away that Mom made the number one best dinner of all time—pasta primavera with homemade spaghetti and vegetarian Caesar salad. Yes!

Henley is dancing in the middle of the kitchen. "Clea's favorite, Clea's favorite. It's your favorite." She points both of her fingers at me and bounces to her own beat.

"You know it," I say, pointing back at her.

Mom is standing next to the stove, stirring sauce and balancing the phone between her ear and shoulder. She isn't saying anything, except, "Totally. I get that," which means she's probably listening to Mel, her roommate from when she lived in New York City. Mom looks up, smiles at me, and points to the empty table. "We're on it," I say.

"Hey, munchkin, help me set things up." I wave Henley over.

"Don't call me that, unless you are thinking about a jelly one. I hate chocolate glazed."

"Since when?"

"I was *bowrn*," she says, hands on her hips.

"Get over here, jelly munchkin."

She smiles and follows my lead. I hand her the forks and napkins, and I carry the plates and knives, and we set the table together.

"Dad!" Henley shouts as soon as he walks into the kitchen.

"Kiddo!" he says, trying to match her enthusiasm, which is impossible for any human. He hugs her and then me. "It smells

30

great." He takes off his tie, kisses Mom hello, then reaches over her shoulder and grabs a piece of the pasta and drops it into his mouth without getting any butter on his blue suit.

"You too," Mom says into the phone and hangs up. She turns around and looks at us. "Thank you, girls, for setting the table."

Henley smiles so big her eyes squeeze together.

Mom tucks her wavy brown hair behind her ears. She picks up the salad and pasta and puts both in the middle of the table, then tells us about her day.

"How was everyone else's day?" Dad asks after we've had a chance to eat. He glances at each of us, waiting for an update. I look into my lap to avoid answering.

"Loose tooth." Henley opens her mouth wide and wiggles one on the bottom. It's hanging by a thread.

"Henley, do you remember what we talked about earlier today?" Mom asks.

She nods her head up and down. "I have a loose tooth." Her voice is so soft, I can barely hear her.

"That's very exciting," Dad says. "I guess it's almost time for the tooth fairy."

Mom and I both scowl at him.

Henley shakes her head and tries as hard as she can to

push back her tears, but they trickle down her chipmunk cheeks. "I don't want that."

"I know." Mom rubs her shoulder softly. "That's why I got you a bag to hang on your door."

It looks like a pillow and says, *Special delivery for the Tooth Fairy only.*

Henley nods, like she remembers.

"Sorry," Dad mouths to Mom. I can't tell if he forgot or if he didn't know. Mom rubs his back with her free hand, which is what she does when she wants us to know that everything is okay, even when it's not.

Dad is away a lot. His job is to buy and fix companies. He's the best problem solver around, which means that every few weeks he's off to a new country or state. But he's always back on Thursday. That's something we can all count on. When he gets home, he tries hard to catch up on everything he missed, but it's impossible, because things happen, little things that are so small they slip away when you aren't looking, and they're the kind of things that don't seem like they even matter, until they do. When you add them all up, they matter a lot.

"How was school?" Dad asks.

It's quiet for a few seconds. I take a big bite of my

primavera, and then another, like I'm so hungry I didn't hear the question.

Henley takes a deep breath. "We're going to a *fawrm* with chicks and cows and pigs." It sounds like she's racing to get the words out, like she's afraid if she doesn't, they might disappear.

There's a fly on the ceiling, circling us, waiting for the best moment to swoop in and join the party. In my head, his name is Floyd.

"That sounds fun," Dad says.

Henley nods.

"What about you?" He looks at me. Floyd lands on the salad bowl.

I shoo him away and watch him fly as fast as he can over to the window where I can't see him anymore.

"Clea, how did it go today?" Dad asks again.

"I beat Sanam in chess," I say, because that's the only part of my day I want to talk about. "She's the best player on our team."

"That's great. What about school?" he asks, glossing over my win like it hardly matters.

"It's actually a really big deal," I say. "I dominated. Red even said so."

Dad looks at Mom. I can tell they're trading secret adult messages.

Floyd is buzzing around us again.

"That stupid fly." Dad swats and misses. Then he stands up and opens the sliding door so Floyd can escape. I wish I could join him. I'd much rather fly around outside and hide in the backyard until this conversation is over.

"Stupid, stupid, stupid," Henley repeats and slurps up the last of her spaghetti.

"Are you finished eating?" Mom asks her.

She nods a lot, like she's a human bobblehead.

"Then you may be excused."

Henley gets up, pushes in her chair, and curtsies. "Did you see?" she asks.

"Very nice," Dad says.

We're all quiet while she makes her way into the other room. Hilda stays sprawled out on top of my feet.

Mom looks at me and puts down her fork. I don't know what's coming, but I can tell it's bad, because she waits for Henley to turn on one of her shows before she says, "Ms. Pumi called."

"Why?" I ask. "What did she say?"

"She's worried about you. She said you came to class unprepared. You didn't do your homework. Is that true?"

I stare into my plate, diving deep into swirls of spaghetti and zucchini. It sounds a lot worse when Mom says it out loud.

"You're not in trouble," Dad says. "And Ms. Pumi isn't going to count this grade as long as you do all your work from now on."

"Really?" I ask.

Dad nods. "We want to know what happened."

I shrug. "I messed up and then I tried to fix it and I made it worse."

"Do you think maybe being on the chess team is too much for you right now?" Mom asks.

"NO!" I shout. "How is that even related?"

"I saw you practicing chess problems last night, so I thought that was maybe why you didn't have time to finish math. It's a lot for anyone to take on. I know you love chess, but school has to come first."

"It does," I say. "It won't happen again."

"Okay." Mom nods like she's trying to believe me, but doesn't. Not really. "You can keep playing—for now—as long as you come up with a better plan, because what you have been doing isn't working. You have to finish all of your homework at home."

I nod, because I want to do everything Mom is saying, and I don't know what's wrong with me that I can't.

After dinner, I go back up to my room and start my homework again. I can't give my parents one more reason to take chess away from me, especially since they don't even know what happened in Spanish yet. Only . . . the lights on the ceiling are buzzing, like there's a bee stuck inside, and I keep looking up and then at the clock, instead of reading the questions in front of me. *I need to stop messing up. Now.* I still have math and history and science and my author project. And I'm running out of time. It's already 6:46 p.m., which is almost 7:00 p.m. I wish the clock would stop, even for a few minutes, because I have so much left to do. It's all piling up. And it feels like I can't breathe.

I close my book and take out my English presentation, because I already did the work, and now the only thing I have left to do is practice. I'm standing in the middle of my bedroom, holding up my poster and talking to my imaginary audience, when Henley walks into my room in her *I'm sassy* pajamas.

She runs over and hugs the side of my arm, squeezing with all her strength, like she knows I need something, and she's trying in her own way to make sure I get it. "Hilda is sleeping in here."

"She likes your room better," I say.

"We *shawre*."

"Not tonight." I want to say yes, but I know Henley needs Hilda more than I do, and not because of the tooth fairy. A few weeks ago, I heard Henley tell Hilda that she's supposed to be talking out loud more at school and that she thinks it might be easier for her to do that if they practice together before bed. I don't want to take that away from her.

Henley kisses me on the cheek and then skips over to the door.

"Good night," I say.

I finish practicing my presentation and then plod through my homework.

When Mom knocks a few hours later, she's wearing a T-shirt and sweatpants with her hair pulled back, like she's ready for bed.

I look at my phone. It's 9:00 and I still have so much to do.

"How's everything going?" Mom asks, standing in the doorway.

"Almost done," I say, because I know that's the right answer.

"That's great. Do you need Dad or me to help with anything?"

I shake my head. "No, thanks."

"Okay. Get some rest."

"I will," I say. "Good night."

As soon as Mom walks away, I stand up, turn my desk lamp on and the ceiling lights off, and close the door to my bedroom. In case Mom decides to check on me again, I use an old sweatshirt to cover the small crack between the bottom of the door and the rug so the light doesn't shine into the hall.

By the time I finally finish my homework and climb under the covers, it's really late. I'm tired and out of it. I set my alarm and stare at the ceiling, but I can't fall asleep. I don't even know how long I try before I give up and turn on an episode of *Sabrina the Teenage Witch*, which is one of my favorite shows. Red and I both love anything with witches and wacky plots.

I guess we both like the idea of having magical powers to fix our problems.

THREE.

THE NEXT MORNING, Mom shakes me awake. "CLEA!" She sounds scared. "How are you not up yet? It's seven fifteen! We have to leave right now."

"NO!" I shout and jump out of bed. School starts in a half hour. There are piles of books and papers covering the floor. I was supposed to wake up early and go over my presentation again.

"I don't understand why this is so difficult. You got up on time yesterday and last week." She shakes her head. "What happened to your alarm?"

I pick up my phone and open the clock, because I'm afraid that maybe Mom is right and I didn't even set it. But it's worse. My alarm is on and ready to wake me up at 6:15 *p.m.* Before I have a chance to explain, she says, "I'm taking your sister to school and then I'm coming back to get you. Please be downstairs in ten minutes. I can't be late. I have an appointment with a student this morning." She walks out of my room, and the bracelets stacked all the way up her arm jangle together, ringing in my ears.

I run into the bathroom, turn on the shower, and let the warm water wash over me. It helps a little. I get dressed and pack my bag as fast as I can, checking to make sure I have everything that's due today, including the poster for my presentation.

The air outside is cooler than I want it to be. The morning sun finds its way through the layers of clouds and pine trees, but it's not as strong as it was even a few weeks ago, when a tiny glimmer felt like a warm cozy blanket. I should have grabbed a jacket on my way out, and I think my sneakers from last year are too small, because they keep rubbing against my heel. But it's too late to go back in the house and start over.

It's a six-minute ride to school, which is exactly enough time to review my project, but I don't want Mom to ask questions, so instead I stare out the window, watching the houses and trees go by.

"What happened?" Mom asks, turning down the radio so the voices sound like they're buzzing and humming somewhere far away.

I shrug, because I want to pretend I set my alarm for the right time.

"Tell me something," she says, trying again.

"I messed up! Okay?" My words come out a little too loud.

"There's no reason to raise your voice. All I want to do is help you."

"I'm sorry," I say, because it's not her fault that I need to do everything better.

Mom reaches out to me without taking her eyes off the road.

I move my hand closer to hers so she can wrap her fingers around mine. Her skin is soft and warm and she holds on, like she's going to protect me. "You're okay," she says. "You made a mistake. It happens to everyone. Let's just move on."

"Okay," I say.

Like it's that easy.

When I get out of the car, the bell rings. I walk quickly down the path and straight through the courtyard into school. I can't be late for English.

When I get to Mr. Lee's room, I'm winded and my heart is racing. It seems like everyone else is relaxed and ready to go. I sit in the front and try to stop replaying all the things I did wrong so far today, because I need to be my best in school and chess. I can't mess up anymore.

I take a long, deep breath to calm myself down, and immediately realize I forgot deodorant! I check the front pocket of my bag to make sure my secret stash is there. It is! *Phew.* I just have to get through the rest of class before I can go to the bathroom with my backpack.

When Mr. Lee walks into the room, I raise my hand. "Could I present first?" I ask as soon as he calls on me.

"Absolutely. Come on up."

I unroll my timeline, which includes every single thing anyone would ever want to know about S. E. Hinton. I take a deep breath. I can do this. "Susan Eloise Hinton was born in Tulsa, Oklahoma, on July 22, 1948, which makes her astrological sign Cancer." I added that part in for pizzazz. "Her first novel, *The Outsiders*, was published in 1967 by Viking when she was only seventeen years old. She decided to go by S. E. instead of Susan Eloise because the narrator of the book is a boy." I'm feeling confident and prepared the whole time I'm presenting, and when I get to the end, I know

I did a great job making my oral biography informative and relatable.

Quinn raises her hand. She's sitting in the second row next to Vivi, looking super fancy and wearing a lot of makeup, like she's trying really hard to remind everyone that she's still important, even though she's not the most popular girl in our grade anymore. She hasn't been ever since Vivi moved here last year from Brazil. Quinn acts like she's okay being second-in-command, but she used to be way more casual and nice before Vivi. I wasn't expecting questions, but I feel prepared to answer basically anything, so I call on her.

"Why did you pick S. E. Hinton?" She twirls the end of her long, blond ponytail.

"I think it's awesome that she wrote such a successful novel at a young age."

"But we're not reading her book in class, so you did it wrong. *The Outsiders* was on the free reading list." Quinn smirks.

Vivi covers her mouth, acting like she's trying not to laugh.

"Clea," Mr. Lee says. "Let's talk more after class." His voice is soft, but really everyone in the room knows I'm in trouble, which means that pretty soon the entire grade will, too, because . . . *hello, that's how things work.*

I grab my poster and sit down as fast as I can, wishing I could melt into my chair like a stick of butter.

When the bell rings, I stay where I am and stare at the floor. We only got halfway through the presentations today, which means if I had waited, instead of volunteering to go first, like an idiot, I would have had time to redo my entire project before Mr. Lee and everyone else found out I did it wrong.

Mr. Lee sits down next to me. His secret T-shirt today says *Wicked.* "I can tell how much time and effort you put into your work." He points to my poster. "You gave it your all." I look up at him, because it seems like maybe whatever he's about to say isn't going to be that bad. "But you didn't follow the directions—and that's a big problem." I swallow hard. "Unfortunately, I have to give you an F."

No. This isn't happening. I can't fail.

"Since this is the first big assignment of the year, I am going to let you present a different author on Friday. I'll give you a new grade and deduct a letter." He opens up the reading list and underlines the sentence at the top of the page that says *Here is a list of books we will be reading and discussing in class this year.*

"Okay. Thank you," I say, because even though the last

thing I want is to get back up and try again in front of everyone, it's the only way I won't get an F.

After school, I go straight to the multipurpose room for chess. We're practicing with the sixth-grade team today. Mr. Lee starts by teaching a new strategy and then he splits us into two groups for a few rounds of human chess.

I'm standing on the life-size board dressed up as one of the white knights. There aren't enough players for a full set, so we're using big plastic pieces in place of pawns. Everyone else is positioned on the giant green and white squares, playing the back rank, except for Sanam and Red, who are on the sidelines, because they're the team captains. Sanam is playing black and Red is white.

The air in the room is stale and sticky. It smells like rubber. I adjust my itchy paper helmet without taking it off my head, because that's against the rules and I can't get eliminated for failing to follow simple directions. I need to do everything possible to stay in the game and prove that I'm good.

The first two rounds go by fast. I move when I'm told, and I don't mess anything up. But I'm too distracted by my costume to call out ideas and help us win.

We only have one round left, and I need to stop rubbing my forehead and focus on the game, because I know I'm only making the itchiness worse, but it's impossible to think about anything other than how uncomfortable my skin feels and how much I want to scratch.

"C6," Sanam says, because she wants her pawn to move ahead one square.

Every square has coordinates. The columns—called files—are labeled A through H, and the rows—called ranks—are labeled 1 through 8.

Quinn follows Sanam's directions and moves the pawn in front of her forward one square. She rolls her eyes so hard, like she wants everyone on both teams to know she thinks Sanam's move is weak and she's not impressed. I think Quinn is jealous of Sanam and everyone who's good at chess, because at the beginning of last year, Quinn was the best player on our team, and by the end, she wasn't even in the top twelve. She was only an alternate. Not that there's anything wrong with being an alternate. I'd love to be in that position, but I'd be pretty mad if the rest of the team kept getting better and I was the same.

It's the white team's turn and Red hasn't said anything. Every few seconds, he pushes his copper hair out of his eyes and walks along the edge of the board. Since anyone on the team is allowed to help, I look around, turning in every direction, trying to figure out the best way to win, because I want to prove I'm ready to compete in the next tournament and be someone who matters to the team.

The game is a lot different from this angle, which I know is the point. It takes me time to adjust, but once I do, I start to see patterns in the pieces. There's a rush of energy that flows through me, taking over my body. The cardboard helmet doesn't feel that bad anymore. I almost forget it's there. I'm focused on finding the answer. I can't shift gears or think about anything other than what's happening on the board until—I got it! I know how to win. "Red," I shout. "Move me. You have to move me to g5."

"*Eerrrrrrrnnnntttt.* Wrong answer," Dylan says. He's standing a few squares away, dressed as the white king, making an X with his arms.

"I'm right," I say, because I'm 100 percent sure.

Red looks at me and then at the board, like he's trying to see what I see without asking questions that might give away my strategy.

"Dude, move the queen to h7. It's the only option." Dylan acts like he's better than everyone because his older brother is a Candidate Master, which means he's good and almost a Master, even though that actually has nothing to do with Dylan.

Red nods. "Yeah. That works," he says, like he's going to listen to Dylan and not to me, even though I'm right.

"No, it doesn't." I try to keep my voice down, but it still sounds so loud compared to everyone else's.

"How would you know?" Dylan looks at me, like I'm gum stuck to the bottom of his brand-new sneaker. "It's not like you've ever played in a tourney."

His words cut into me. I bite down on my lip, because he's wrong about the next move and me. Everything I'm feeling is bubbling up.

"Kg5 is just dumb, like you," he says.

"Actually, it's how you win—Kg5. *Then* Qh7. Checkmate." The words fly out of my mouth, bouncing off the gym walls and back at me, before I can think about what I'm doing and stop myself.

"Wow," Quinn says. "Way to freak out and ruin the game."

Everyone laughs.

"That's enough," Mr. Lee says. "I expect all of you to be supportive of one another, even when you're playing on opposite sides of the board." He pauses, then looks at me. "Strong

48

chess players need to stay calm and composed. I'd like you to work on that."

I want to tell him that I didn't mean to blurt out the answer. I don't know what happened. But I'm afraid if I say anything right now, I'll cry, and I can't, so I look down at the floor. I need to never do anything like that ever again.

"Okay. Let's continue where we left off," Mr. Lee says. "Red, it's still your move. And it's probably best not to go with Kg5, Qh7."

I keep my head down and stare at my sneakers, wishing I had the power to make myself disappear.

"Qh7," Red says.

"Boom. In your face," Dylan says in this cool-guy way, like he could be talking to anyone, but I know he's talking to me.

I don't look up at him or say anything. I'm frozen.

It only takes Sanam a few moves to beat us. When the match is finally over, Mr. Lee says, "Please come to practice tomorrow focused and ready to play your best."

Everyone puts away their props as fast as possible and races out of the room, like the awkwardness permeating the air is actually toxic. Quinn scurries by me and over to Vivi, who's waiting for her by the door, leaning against the wall in her field hockey gear. Her lips are perfectly glossed and her black ponytail falls down her back in a never-ending maze of shiny tendrils.

Quinn whispers something in Vivi's ear, but she doesn't take her eyes off me, like she wants to make it clear that they're talking about how I ruined the game. Everyone is.

I take off my helmet, drop it in the basket with the other costumes, and turn around. Red is standing by the water fountain waiting for me. I walk over to him.

"That was really bad. I don't know what happened." I look at him, like maybe he has the answer.

"You're the only one who knew how to win," he says, trying as hard as he can to make what I did okay. "I'm sorry I didn't listen to you. You were right. I couldn't see the next move until you said it."

I shake my head, because he shouldn't be sorry. It's not Red's fault that I blurted out the answer and gave away the game.

"You say whatever pops into your head. That's your thing. Don't worry. It'll blow over."

"Chess? Or English?"

"Both." He looks away like he's sorry he knows what happened in class.

"Who told you?" I ask, even though I'm pretty sure I already know the answer.

"Dylan," he says.

I hate Dylan, but I don't say that, because Red doesn't. They're friends.

"Did you really do the entire project wrong?"

"Pretty much." I nod. "I'm so dumb."

"Don't talk about my best friend like that," he says. "It's not cool. You made a mistake. That doesn't make you stupid."

"Yeah, sure. At least Mr. Lee is letting me redo the assignment on Friday, aka not giving me an F."

"Phew. You'll do an awesome job, and then you'll crush everyone in chess, and no one will remember today ever happened. It won't matter."

"Do you have a backup plan in case that doesn't work?" I ask.

"Obviously. I'm all over it," he says. "I'll embarrass myself and give them something else to talk about."

"And how exactly are you going to do that?" I ask.

"I hadn't gotten that far," he says. "But we won't need a backup plan. It'll be okay. I promise. You can do it."

I want to believe him.

Red's mom drives me home from school on Tuesdays and Wednesdays.

When I walk through the front door, Hilda starts barking. "Clea," Mom says. "Can you please come in here?"

I follow Mom's voice into the living room. She's sitting next to Dad on the fancy embroidered sofa that no one ever uses. They're both stiff and buttoned up in their work clothes, which is so not normal or good for me. Dad definitely shouldn't be home right now. I think about turning around and bolting out the door, but I know that will only delay whatever is about to happen.

I sink into the blue velvet chair across from my parents.

They're looking at me like they're waiting for me to speak. For once, I don't have anything to say.

Henley runs into the living room and grabs on to my arm. I can tell she wants to show me something.

"Henley, honey, Dad and I need to talk to Clea alone for a few minutes."

"How many is a few?" Henley asks.

"I'll let you know when we're finished."

Henley looks at me, her forehead scrunching up.

"It's okay," I whisper, because I don't want her to worry.

She hugs my arm and dashes out of the room.

Mom takes a deep breath. "Dad and I met with Ms. Curtis

this afternoon. She's the middle school learning specialist."

I know who Ms. Curtis is, but I don't say that—or anything. "Over the past week, a few of your teachers have expressed concerns about how you're doing in school this year and—"

"I know what happened with the author project sounds bad and like a really big deal, because I got an F for now, but I swear it's not. I made one stupid mistake with the directions. And the grade isn't permanent. I'm redoing the presentation on Friday, and I already picked a new author. I'm going to fix the whole thing."

"It is a big deal." Mom sounds mad. "You did the assignment wrong. We've talked about this. You need to read the instructions carefully and pay attention to what is being asked of you so you don't make careless mistakes. This is what you were working on with Chloe-Louise this summer."

I hate how she's explaining what happened, like I don't already know all the things I did wrong.

"I know!" I shout. "I didn't mean to mess up. I won't do it again. Okay?"

Mom sighs and then looks at Dad, like she's had enough.

"We know you didn't, Clea," Dad says. "But at this point,

53

we need to get to the bottom of what's going on at school and come up with a plan to help you. Based on the problems you've been having finishing your assignments, following directions, and speaking out of turn—"

"How is that related? Oh, wait—it's not."

"Please stop interrupting," Dad says.

"Stop being wrong," I say back, because it feels like they're rewriting everything that happened to make it matter more than it does.

Then Dad tells me, "Your teachers think it's important that we have you evaluated for attention-deficit/hyperactivity disorder."

"ADHD? You can't be serious right now!" I keep waiting for them to smile or laugh or do something to show that they're joking, but they just sit there staring at me, like they're totally serious.

"This is what your school is recommending. And we're taking their guidance," Dad says. "You're going to have an assessment, which means that Ms. Curtis will attend some of your classes tomorrow, and then once we get an appointment, you'll be out two or three days for testing."

"I can't miss three days. I'll get so far behind. And I'm definitely not skipping chess. No way. That's not happening.

I need to be at practice. It's important. I actually have a chance to play in the next tournament."

"I really don't think Mr. Lee is going to penalize you for not being at chess when you'll be out for tests that the school suggested," Mom says.

"You don't know that," I say back.

"We understand how much you love chess," Mom says. "But it can't get in the way of school."

"It's not! No—just, no. I don't have ADHD. I can sit in my chair, and I can focus. During chess, for example, I'm super focused. I'm like a focus machine."

"Not everyone with ADHD is hyperactive," Mom says.

I roll my eyes. "That literally makes no sense."

"It's complicated, which is why we want to make sure we have the right information."

"So this is happening? Even if I say no?"

Mom and Dad both nod.

"Can you schedule the test on a Thursday and Friday so I don't miss chess?"

"We'll see," Mom says. "It's not so easy to get an appointment, and we're doing everything we can to make this happen as soon as possible."

"Chess is the only thing I'm actually good at. I don't get why you're trying to take it away from me."

Mom shakes her head. "We're not. We're trying to fix what's happening in school."

"I keep messing up. That's what's happening. It doesn't matter what you do. You can't fix that. I just need to work harder."

Mom looks at me like she doesn't know what to say.

"We really think you need this, Clea," Dad says.

"Just don't blame me when it turns out I don't have ADHD, and I got even further behind and missed chess for nothing." I stomp upstairs to my room and slam the door. Then I take out my phone and call Red over and over until he finally answers.

"Are you okay?" he asks as soon as he picks up.

"Not really." My voice is shaky. "I'm going to be out of school and chess for two or maybe three days, because my parents are making me get tested for ADHD."

"You can't. Mr. Lee hates when people don't show up to practice. If one person isn't there, he has to play."

"My parents don't care about chess," I say. "All they want to do is come up with a stupid plan that's not going to fix anything."

"I'm sorry," he says. "You obviously don't have ADHD. I think they basically test everyone who gets bad grades for it now. It's like a thing or whatever. But I don't know, maybe a plan could be good. It might help. You could get extra time on tests and other stuff that would make school easier."

"You think I need a plan?" I ask.

"I don't know. The end of last year was bad. And so far, this year . . ."

I know Red isn't trying to be mean. I just wish it didn't hurt so much.

"When's the test?" he asks.

"I'm not sure. It can be hard to get an appointment."

"That's great. The longer it takes, the better. You'll have time to show everyone how good you are at chess before you skip out on practice. And if you keep winning, Mr. Lee will play you. You probably won't even miss one tournament."

"I didn't think of that," I say.

"Dude, where are you?" someone asks in the background. It sounds like Dylan, which doesn't make sense, because Red isn't allowed to have friends over on school nights.

"I gotta go," Red says. "Don't worry. It'll work out."

"Okay. Thanks." It helps to hear Red say that he thinks I could still play in all the tournaments, even if I have to miss chess. As long as it takes a while to get an appointment, the one thing I'm good at *isn't* going to get taken away from me.

FOUR.

I WAKE UP early and start my day with all the things I love: chess and magic and toast with crunchy peanut butter. I need to do everything I can think of to make sure that today is better than yesterday.

I put on an episode of *Bewitched* that I've seen so many times I practically know it by heart. I only sort of listen to the show while I practice tactics on my computer. I'm in the zone, but it feels good to have Samantha's voice in the background, like she's an old friend with magical powers hanging around my room to keep me company.

I press *next* on my screen and a new problem appears. The computer moves the black queen from d1 to d4. Right away I know that I'm playing white and that my king is in trouble. I need to either take out the black queen or protect my king.

My eyes scan the pieces on the screen in front of me, like I'm a spy looking for clues. Finally, I figure it out. I move my knight to d4 and capture the queen.

Solved! appears on the screen. I smile to myself, because it feels good to win.

I press *next* and jump into a new situation. It's tricky. But I recognize the pattern immediately, and I know what to do.

I've won five in a row when Mom opens the door to my room without knocking. "Oh, um, hi," she says, like she's surprised to see me dressed and ready to go.

"What's up?" I ask, even though it's obvious that she thought I was still sleeping.

"I came to check on you." She walks over and sits down next to me, smelling like lavender and fresh laundry.

"One of the doctors I called yesterday—Dr. Gold—had a last-minute cancellation and the other people on her waiting list couldn't take the appointment. Not all psychiatrists do evaluations but Dr. Gold does. She thinks we can have a consultation and complete the testing in two days—next Monday and Tuesday. Isn't that great?"

"Wait—what? No." I'm doing everything I can to not scream, because I know Mom won't listen to me if I start yelling. That's a rule in our house. And I need her to hear what I'm saying. "Please. Don't make me go. Our first tournament is next Saturday. I need to prove myself before I miss practice."

Mom looks confused. "I thought you'd be happy to get this done in two days and sorted out at the beginning of the season, when the matches don't matter as much."

"You made that up! That's not a thing." My voice comes out too loud. "Please cancel the appointment. I don't want to get behind in chess and then have to catch up. I'm already doing that in everything else. I want to keep winning."

"I can't do that, Clea. Her next opening isn't for months. We need to figure out what's going on as soon as possible. I can call Mr. Lee and talk to him. I'm sure he'll make an exception and let you play in the tournament. You're only missing two days."

That's when I realize Mom has no clue how the team works or what it takes to get to compete in tournaments. She thinks chess is some cute hobby that doesn't matter, when it means everything to me. "I should be the one to talk to Mr. Lee," I say. "He's my coach. I want him to know I'm responsible and serious about chess."

"Great idea." She smiles at me, so at least I know she'll stay out of it.

When I get to school, Red is waiting for me at our bench like always. I drop my backpack and sit down next to him. "The ADHD test is on Monday and Tuesday."

"I thought it was supposed to take a while," he says.

"Me too. But I guess not. I need to tell Mr. Lee today."

"I'll go with you. I can back you up. Tell him how good you are and stuff."

"I'm not letting you do that," I say. "He likes you."

"He likes you, too."

I roll my eyes.

Red goes on. "Mr. Lee is all about players who work hard and win—aka you. You've already won one match, and if you win two more times, you're going to get picked."

"I've never won three matches in a row," I say.

"You've never had to." He grins.

"That's true." I smile back, because he's right. I don't have a choice.

After the bell rings, I go straight to math. Ms. Curtis is there, sitting in the back of the room by the door. She pins her honey-colored hair off her pale white face and fans herself with her notes. I accidentally make eye contact with her, and then glance away as fast as I can. I don't want anyone to figure out that she's here for me. It's embarrassing enough that I bombed my author project. The last thing I need is for everyone in our grade to find out that the school thinks there's something wrong with me.

I walk to the front of the room and pick a seat by the window, really far away from Ms. Curtis. I do my best not to look at her too many times, even though I really want to know how I'm doing and I can't help myself or stop my head from turning. Also, I wonder if she's been staring at me the entire time, making it super obvious why she's here, or if she's actually playing it cool. I know that pretty soon she's going to figure out that I don't have ADHD. Eventually it will be clear, and even though I already know I'm not smart and that's the reason I keep messing up, I think it will be a lot harder for me once everyone else knows.

After math, I have history and then Spanish. Ms. Curtis is in the back of each of those classes, too. The only good part of the day so far is that Señora Campo decides not to count the pop quiz, because a lot of people didn't do their best, which is awesome news for me. I peek a bunch of times to see what Ms. Curtis is doing—mostly writing things down in her notebook and looking around the room and then back at me.

When I get to the lab, Ms. Curtis isn't there, like maybe she's finally done being my super stalker.

Dr. Kapoor explains the experiment we're going to be doing in class today, and then she lets us pick our partners. The second she's finished explaining the instructions I walk as fast as I can over to Sanam, because she's smart and good at everything in school. On my way to her desk, I accidentally bump into the corner of a table. It hurts, but I keep moving until I'm standing next to her. "Do you want to work together?"

"I was going to ask you the same thing," she says, which is cool, but also weird, because if I were Sanam, I would never want to work with me.

We walk over to an empty station, divide the list of supplies in half, and split up to collect everything faster. Once we have all the materials, I read the directions out loud and Sanam follows along. She measures the correct amount of agar and water and stirs the mixture. Then we both walk over to the microwave and wait in line until it's our turn to boil the solution. When we get back to our station, we have to wait for the agar-and-water mixture to cool before we can pour it into petri dishes.

Quinn walks over to our table. "I have a question," she announces, like she's going to ask us about something related to the lab. Instead she leans in and whispers, "So who do you think it is?" She glances across the room to where Ms. Curtis is sitting, writing in her notebook. I wonder how long she's been in the corner like that, scribbling away. "Any guesses?" She looks right at me. My heart starts pounding.

"No clue." I try to sound confident, but don't.

"Well, I've narrowed it down to Jack and the two of you," she says, tapping her pencil against her notebook, like she's really put a lot of thought into her investigation. "You're the only ones who have been in every single class she's been trailing. Other than me, but I'm smart. So, no."

"I'm pretty sure we would know if we were being watched," I say back, because I've already decided I'm going to deny that it's me to anyone who asks. Even though I think I could trust Sanam to keep a secret, I can't take that kind of chance right now.

"Mmm, probably not." Quinn shakes her head. "Last year, I heard someone, who will remain nameless, was getting evaluated for multiple days before the teachers told that person."

"How do you know that?" I ask.

"I'm really good at figuring out people's secrets. It's sort of

65

a talent." She twirls the end of her hair. "Want to know who I think it is?" Her eyebrows go straight up, and I'm not sure if I want to know what she's thinking right now, so I don't say yes, but I don't look away from her, either. I keep waiting for her to say, *Everyone knows it's you.*

She looks right at me and whispers, "Too bad. I guess you'll just have to wait and see." Then she turns around and walks back to her table.

I pick up the mixture and start pouring the liquid into the petri dishes, because I'm pretty sure that's the next step, and I want to go back to working on the lab and forget about everything that happened with Quinn.

"Want to know who I think it is?" Sanam asks.

I look at her. "Sure." My voice cracks.

She mouths, "Quinn," without letting any sound escape.

I want to ask Sanam why she thinks that, because Quinn always gets good grades. Only I know I need to change the subject, since I'm the one who's actually being evaluated. I pick up the marker and hand it to her. "Your writing is better than mine. Can you do the labeling?"

"Um, okay," she says, like she was expecting me to say something else, and I'm afraid I've accidentally made it obvious that it's me.

* * *

When I get to last period, Ms. Curtis is already sitting in the corner of the multipurpose room, like she thinks no one can see her and her stupid notebook. Jack doesn't play chess, which means the list of possible suspects has been cut down to three—Sanam, Quinn, and me.

There's a pairing list taped to the wall, like at a real tournament. Most of the team is crowded around the piece of paper. I walk over and scan the names, looking for mine. I hope I'm playing white this match. Something about having the first move makes me feel like the game is mine, and my opponent

SEVENTH-GRADE MOCK TOURNAMENT

BOARD #	WHITE	BLACK
1	Becker, Ella	Cohen, Mateo
2	Verma, Pari	Jones, Hunter
3	Patel, Ajay	Marino, Lily
4	Levine, Red	Nasimi, Sanam
5	McClaran, Quinn	Andrews, Isaac
6	Howard, Harrison	Goodman, Ethan
7	Adams, Clea	Johnson, Dylan
8	Brown, Joshua	Shah, Layla
9	Dalton, Isabelle	Smith, Wyatt
10	Kim, Charles	Walsh, Emily

better watch out. Before I break the news to Mr. Lee that I'm missing chess next week, I need to prove I can help the team win.

I'm playing white. *YES!* And Dylan. *UGH.* I need to ignore him and win.

Board #7 is okay. I mean, it's not great. It would be better if I were at board #1-6. But it's definitely not horrible. I take my seat and look at the pieces in front of me. I try to visualize my opening and think through all the moves I'm going to use to take charge.

"Well, this should be easy." Dylan sits down across from me, pushes his hair out of his eyes, and smiles, showing off his dimples, which would be cute if he weren't such a jerk all the time.

I don't say anything back, because I know he's trying to throw me off so I don't play my best.

"It's too bad you're missing practice next week," he says. "There's no chance you'll ever play in a tourney now."

How does he know that?

"Don't look so worried. Red didn't tell me why you're going to be out. Not that I care. He just asked me to take it easy on you, which I'm clearly not doing."

"Good," I shoot back. "I don't need your pity."

"You kind of do. I mean, even Red thinks so, and he's your only friend."

"Well, he's wrong." I really hope Dylan can't tell how much his words hurt.

"So why are you going to be out?" he asks.

"Why do you care?" I sound as angry as I am, and not because of Dylan. He's always rude to me. I'm mad at Red for telling him that I'm missing chess and for thinking I couldn't beat Dylan on my own.

"I didn't before, but now that it's a big mystery I need to know."

"Good luck with that," I say.

"I don't need luck." He smirks. "I have sources."

Mr. Lee claps his hands to get our attention. "I want everyone to stay focused and give this game your all. Let's get to work."

I take a deep breath and zone in on the board. Dylan taps the clock. I focus on making the easy moves first, developing my pawns, my knights, queen, and bishops. That's the only way I'm going to win. I try to imagine my plan playing out before Dylan makes his next move to save on time. I stay aware of his choices and double-check that all my pieces are safe. Every

time I make a move, I repeat the same words in my head—
Move. Let go. Tap. Write.

My opening is solid, and I only need extra time figuring out one of my moves. I still have eight minutes to win. I'd rather have eleven like Dylan, but I think I can beat him in the time I have left.

The only problem is that I need to distract him so he doesn't notice my knight making its way to the other side of the board.

I move my bishop on the king's side up one square on the diagonal, let go of the piece, and hit the timer as fast as I can.

Dylan does exactly what I want. He moves his pawn up one square, then taps the clock. I wonder if he knows what I'm doing and has a bigger plan, or if he's actually falling for it. I move my knight up and over, capturing the pawn he just moved and setting myself up to win.

Dylan moves his knight over two and down one, next to mine.

I castle king-side, which means my king slides over and swaps places with my rook, tap the clock, and glance at the time—four minutes left. I can do this. I can win.

He takes my bishop out with his knight, and I take his knight out with my queen.

Then he sends his bishop across the board, like he's ready to take out my knight.

It's hot in the room, and I'm sweating under too many layers. Winning is taking longer than I expected. I'm running out of time. I move my knight up and over, cornering Dylan into checkmate.

I did it. I won!

I take a long deep breath and fall back into my chair, letting the happy victory feeling sink in and take over. Everything is going to work out. That's when I realize—I forgot to stop the timer!

I pull myself up as fast as I can and slam my hand against the clock. Only I'm too afraid to look. I can't be out of time or I'll lose the match.

"You still won," Dylan says. I keep waiting for him to follow up with something rude. Instead he reaches out to shake my hand.

I force myself to look at the clock, because I feel like he's messing with me.

He's not. I won—with twenty seconds left. *Phew.*

"Good game," I say, shaking his hand—it's warm and a little unsteady, like he's nervous or embarrassed or something else that makes me almost feel bad for him . . . until I remember it's Dylan.

"Good game," he says back.

Most of the team is standing on the other side of the multipurpose room. Dylan walks over to Red and whispers something to him—I really hope it's not about me.

"Great win today, Clea," Mr. Lee says.

"Thank you." I can't help but grin. It feels good to be noticed for doing something right. I take a deep breath. This is my chance to tell Mr. Lee about next week. "I just found out that I need to—" I look around to make sure no one else is near us, listening to me. "I'm getting tested for, um, ADHD on Monday and Tuesday, so I'm not going to be at practice. I'm really sorry. I know being out hurts the team, and I don't want to do that. I love chess and I want to play in the tournament so badly. But it was the only appointment for a long time. So I was wondering if maybe you would let me do something extra to make up for it, because I'm ready to play. I know it."

Mr. Lee pauses like he's thinking. "As you know, I always try to do what's in the best interest of the team and that

72

usually means having everyone at every practice." I cross my fingers on both hands and hold my breath, because there's a sinking feeling in my stomach, like he's about to say something that's not good for me and I really don't want him to. "In this case, being tested is more important than being at chess. So I expect that when you're here, you'll give practice your all, and if I see that commitment from you, then I'll make sure you have the same chance of playing in the tournament as everyone else. And I won't hold these absences against you or the team."

I let out all of the air and the fear I've been holding inside. "I'm going to work really hard. I promise."

"Good," he says. "If I were you, I'd take some time over the next few days to practice on my own. There are only eight players who have won two games in a row—soon to be nine." He glances at Quinn and Isaac. "And we aren't playing one-on-one on Monday, which means you're only missing one game. So if you win next Wednesday, you have a good chance of playing in the tournament."

"Really?!" I ask.

He grins. "There are no guarantees, but I think you should be prepared."

"I am! I will be!" I smile so big it hurts.

73

I walk over to the other side of the room. I want to tell Red what Mr. Lee just said, because he was right about everything and I'm so excited. I'm not sure I can hold it in. But I'm too mad at him, so I lean against the empty wall and stare at the floor.

A few minutes later, Red walks over and stands next to me.

"You won," he says. "That's awesome."

"I can't believe you told Dylan that I'm missing practice." I try to keep my voice low, but it doesn't matter that I'm talking softly—I still sound as angry as I am.

"I didn't tell him why," Red says, like that makes it okay. "I just wanted him to go easy on you so you'd win, because you deserve to play in the tournament. And I knew he'd be cool about it, since he's definitely going to win the rest of his games."

"You didn't think there was any chance I could actually beat him on my own?" I ask.

"You know I think you're really good. But his brother is almost a Candidate Master, and he's basically coaching Dylan every night. I think it'd be hard for anyone on the team to beat him."

I hate that no matter what I say right now, Red is going to think Dylan let me win, when he didn't.

I want to tell him what Dylan said to me, but I stop myself, because they're friends now—for real. And I have no idea where that leaves me.

On Friday, Mr. Lee invites me to the front of the room to redo my author presentation. When I stand up, Quinn covers her mouth with both hands, like she's trying not to laugh at me. There are knots in my stomach getting tighter with each step. I need to ignore her. If I get an A on round two, I could end up with a B. That could be okay. I'd still be on the chess team.

I unroll my poster, which is extra happy and glittery thanks to Henley. I do everything I can to not look at Quinn even for a second. She's in the second row on the right side of the room, so I turn to the people sitting on the left and talk directly to them about the only author who no one else picked: Kelly Barnhill. She wrote *The Girl Who Drank the Moon*, which is about magic, aka perfect for me!

Even though I feel a little awkward about how I'm standing, it's okay, because I don't get distracted.

When I'm finished presenting, Mr. Lee says, "Thank you

for sharing about Kelly Barnhill and for giving us such great context for this book." He looks around the room, like he wants to make sure everyone knows I did a good job. I can tell by the way he smiles at me right before I sit down that I probably got an A, or maybe an A+.

After school, I'm sitting on the floor in the family room across the coffee table from Henley, teaching her about "promoting," which is one of the coolest parts of chess, while I wait for Red to get here.

I want to text him and tell him not to bother coming over, because I don't really want to see him tonight. I'm still hurt that he told Dylan I was missing school, and annoyed because all of a sudden it seems like they're best friends, too. But we always hang out on Friday nights. We make pizzas with my dad and watch movies about magic. It's been our thing ever since fourth grade when he moved from Pennsylvania to Massachusetts, and we became BFFs. We were in an achievement club called "magic" where we learned different tricks and talked about Harry Potter. Red and I were the only ones who picked magic as our number one choice. Everyone else was a hater who didn't get into the club they really wanted, so we stuck together, and we have ever since. But now I'm afraid if I tell him not to come over, I'll push him even further away.

I clear my throat. Hilda sits up, ears at attention, and then collapses into a fluffy ball by Henley's feet.

Henley looks at the chessboard between us, like she's confused. "Where are all the pieces I like? No horses. Or anything good." She crosses her arms and huffs.

"They already got captured," I say. "I'm going to teach you an end-of-game strategy."

Her blue eyes look empty and glossed over, like she has no clue what I'm talking about, but doesn't want me to know that.

"You're going to learn how to win," I clarify.

"Winning!" she says. "Like you."

I smile. "This is a passed pawn." I point to the white pawn that is on its way to the other side of the board. "It has no enemy pawns in front of it or on either side, so it can move straight ahead on the file, one square at a time, without being captured."

"Boring." She crosses her arms. "Pawns are slowpokes."

"Don't underestimate them. Pawns are important," I say as confidently as I can. I want Henley to believe me, because it's true. "When a passed pawn gets all the way to the other end of the board, it can turn into a different piece—any one you want."

"No way!"

"Way!" I say.

"Pawns are cool! *Abwa-cadabwa*." She points to the board, holding up an imaginary wand. "Poof. You're a horse."

"I know you like the knights the best," I say, "but most of the time you're going to want to turn your pawn into a queen."

"Duh," she says. "The queen moves fastest."

"Exactly." I try not to sound surprised, even though I am. I mean, I know she listens to me, but I didn't realize until right now that sometimes when I'm with Henley it feels like I'm the queen, because anything I say goes.

I finish showing Henley a few other ways that pawns can help win the game, and then Red walks through the front door. He plops down on the sofa. "Want to watch *Hocus Pocus* with us tonight?" he asks Henley, like everything is fine and the same, even though it's not.

Henley shakes her head, looking down at the carpet. She doesn't want him to know she's afraid of witches.

She keeps her eyes down and shuffles over to me.

I hug her. "Thanks for playing chess."

"Welcome," she whispers and then disappears down the hall with Hilda.

I usually love Friday nights the best, because Red is here and pizza is my number one favorite food and Dad is always home. His suitcase is unpacked and hidden in the back of the closet where it belongs, and I can almost trick myself into believing that he'll be home forever. But tonight doesn't feel like a Friday because Dad is still at his office, so we had to order pizza, and I sort of wish Red would leave.

"So, um, what do you think your test is going to be like?" Red asks.

I shrug and look down at the board between us. "No clue." I start putting away the pawns, hoping my answer is enough to get him to change the subject, because for the first time, there's a big important thing that's happening to me and I don't want to talk about it—not with Red.

"What do you think they're going to have you do? Like how will they definitely know you have it?"

"I don't know."

"Why are you being weird?" he asks.

"I'm not," I say, even though I know I am. I don't want to tell Red anything about me anymore, because he might tell Dylan. And even though I get that he was trying to help me play in the tournament, it feels like he thinks I'm not good enough to be picked on my own or to be his only best friend. And I want to say everything I'm thinking right now, like before, like always, so he can tell me all the reasons I'm wrong and promise he'll never talk to Dylan about me again. Only, I'm too afraid he won't. Or worse—he'll say everything I want to hear and it will sound like a lie.

I know I need to say something, because we're just sitting here in silence. "I'm nervous, and I guess I'm trying not to think about it," I say, because that's true, too, and easier, and right now, I don't need anything else to feel hard.

He nods, like he gets what that feels like. "It will be okay. I know it. The test will help, and they'll make a plan, then everything will go back to the way it was before."

I really hope he's right.

ON MONDAY MORNING, Mom is supposed to drive Henley to school and then bring me to Dr. Gold's office. When we get to the front of the drop-off line, Mom parks, gets out of the car, and walks over to Henley's teacher, Mrs. McPhee. I can't tell what Mom is saying, because she's facing away from me, but she keeps pointing at Henley, who's standing next to her best friends, the Ellies, and looking at the ground with her shoulders slumped over, like she wants to disappear. I always forget about the shy, scared version of my sister until she's right in front of me.

A few minutes later, Mom gets back in the car and sighs. It's the loud kind that sounds like a roar.

"Everything okay?" I ask.

"School is just really hard for your sister, and I hate that teacher. I need everyone to be focused on helping Henley right now, before her problem gets bigger and it's even harder for her to communicate. I don't know if she doesn't care or she can't see it, but it's so aggravating." Mom takes a deep breath. She turns the car back on and starts driving. I wonder if she ever gets that mad for me.

Dr. Gold's office is one town over in a pink Victorian house with white shutters and a big front porch that feels far away from my real life and all the people who know me and are on their way to school right now.

Mom parks at the end of the long gravel driveway, and I follow her up the porch stairs, through the front door, and into an empty waiting room. There's no place to check in, like at my regular doctor, just five closed doors. One is the bathroom and the other four have signs with different names. I pick a chair across from the door that says DR. LILLIAN S. GOLD, and Mom sits next to me. She takes one of the crinkly magazines stacked on the side table and flips through the glossy pages. I stare at the ceiling. She hasn't said anything about our appointment all morning, and even though I'm getting nervous and it would probably help to talk, even about something else, I'm not going to start now. The only thing I want to talk or think about is chess, and she doesn't care.

After almost ten minutes of waiting, Dr. Gold's office door finally opens, and she pops her head out. She looks right at me and smiles. She's wearing a dress with yellow streaks that reminds me of mustard and looks pretty against her dark brown skin. "I'm Dr. Gold. You must be Clea and Clea's mom." Her voice is low and scratchy and I sort of want her to keep talking, because everything she says sounds like a song. "Come on in whenever you're ready." She leaves the door open and her long braids fall down her back, swaying as she moves.

Inside her office, it smells like gingerbread. There's a hand-painted sign on the wall that reads: *No one can make you feel inferior without your consent. —Eleanor Roosevelt.* There are three different areas. A small sofa with chairs for talking, a table on the other side of the room, and a desk with a big marble chess set. I wonder if Dr. Gold actually plays, or if the board is there to make her office look important. Red told me that's a thing adults do sometimes.

"Take a seat," she says. "Anywhere you'd like."

I pick the gray leather sofa, and Mom chooses the fuzzy chair closest to the door.

Dr. Gold sits down across from us and looks right at me. "Before we jump in, I want to talk a bit about what we're going to do over the next two days, and then I'm hoping we can chat for a little while. How does that sound to you?"

"Great," Mom says.

Dr. Gold is waiting for me to say something, so I say, "Fine," because I can tell it's not the kind of question I'm supposed to answer honestly.

"Okay." She nods. "You're going to spend time today and tomorrow with one of my colleagues—Dr. Sharma—working on an assessment that will help us understand how you process information. I'd like you to try your best to answer all the questions presented even when you find them to be challenging. Then, on Friday after school, you'll come back here with your parents and we'll talk through the results of the test and evaluation and discuss a plan for how we're going to move forward."

"That's great," Mom says.

"What do you think?" Dr. Gold looks at me.

I shrug.

"I'd really like it if you were honest," she says, tilting her head, like she's trying to find the answer. I'm not really sure if I believe her, or if she's doing that fake-o adult thing, where she's pretending to care what I think. Then she says, "How you feel about being here can impact your evaluation."

"I didn't know that," I say.

She nods again.

Even though I'm scared to get tested and find out how dumb I really am, I don't want to mess things up, so I tell her the truth. "I already know I don't have ADHD, so I think it's stupid that I'm missing school and chess for no reason."

"Clea." Mom says my name like I'm in trouble.

"What? All I did was follow the directions, Mom. You should be happy. I'm usually bad at that, remember? Isn't that why I'm here?"

"You're being rude," Mom says.

"Sorry," I apologize to Dr. Gold, because it's not her fault that I'm mad at Mom. "I was trying to be honest so I didn't ruin your test."

"I'm glad to hear that you don't want to miss school," Dr. Gold says. "That tells me you don't hate being there, which will make this process a lot easier."

"I never thought about that," Mom says.

Dr. Gold looks at me. "Can you tell me why you don't think you have ADHD?"

"I just don't," I say. "I mean, kids in my grade have it, and I'm not really like them. I can sit still. I don't blurt out answers all the time or get out of my seat."

"I understand why the name of the disorder is confusing, but you actually don't have to be hyperactive to have ADHD."

"That makes no sense," I point out, just like I pointed it out when Mom said it.

"Hyperactivity is just one component. It happens to be the most visible, which is why people recognize the symptoms and assume they're the same. But they're not. There are different types of ADHD—hyperactive-impulsive, inattentive, and a combined type. In order to diagnose someone under eighteen, they have to persistently show six symptoms in one of the two categories or in both catagories for at least six months." Dr. Gold looks over at Mom like she wants to make sure she's following along. "And those symptoms need to have been present before age twelve and in two or more settings. There also needs to be clear evidence that the symptoms are interfering with academic or social functioning."

"I still don't think I have it," I say. "I mean, I was totally good at school until the end of last year, *after* I turned twelve."

"I understand," Dr. Gold says.

"And I thought no hyperactivity was called ADD," I say.

"ADD is actually an outdated term. We use a different set of criteria to make a diagnosis now, so the name is different. Basically no one gets diagnosed with ADD anymore."

"Everyone says it wrong," I say.

"I know." She smiles. "I think I have enough information for now. Clea, why don't we chat a bit more on our own, and then I'll take you over to Dr. Sharma's office so you can get started. Mom, we'll see you a little later."

"Why can't you do the test?" I ask.

"That's a great question, Clea," Dr. Gold says. "There are different ways to determine if someone has ADHD. Not everyone takes the exact same test. And based on everything I know about you so far from your parents and teachers, I think it makes sense for us to start with an assessment that has to be administered by a psychologist who is trained to give the test. I'm a psychiatrist, which means I have a different background and education."

"Okay," I say, because even though I'd rather stay with Dr. Gold, I get why I can't.

After Mom leaves, Dr. Gold asks, "Did you say that you play chess?"

I nod. "I'm on the seventh-grade team. I won my first two practice games, which is a really big deal. Only nine people out of twenty did that."

"That's impressive." Dr. Gold sounds like she means it.

"Thanks," I say. "I love playing so much."

"Me too. If you had to pick the most powerful piece on the board, which would you choose?"

"The queen," I say without stopping to think.

"Interesting," she says. "Why?"

"Because she can move backward and forward and on a diagonal in any direction until she runs into another piece."

Dr. Gold nods, like maybe she agrees. She has one of those very still faces where it's hard to tell what she's thinking most of the time. "Is there anything that makes the queen weak?"

I think about her question for a few seconds. "She's pretty much always under attack. If you move the queen out in front, she's vulnerable and needs extra protection, which isn't that great."

"So even though she's the strongest piece on the board, that sometimes puts her in positions where she's the weakest piece in the game?"

"I think that's true," I say.

"Could the weakest piece on the board ever be the strongest?"

"Definitely," I say. "Like a pawn or the king."

"I hadn't thought about the king."

"Really?" I ask. "I mean, the king can't do anything. He's super weak. But he determines the entire game. He holds all the power."

"I like that a lot," she says. "It's all about playing to the piece's strengths. Find the thing it can do that no one else can. Start to think about those negatives as positives, and be prepared for how the positives can be negatives. You have to look at each piece from all the different angles."

"I know we're not talking about chess anymore," I say.

She grins. "You're missing important parts of your regular day to be here, and that's hard, so I want you to understand why you're being asked to do that. I'm not just looking to see if you have ADHD. I'm trying to identify as many of your strengths and challenges as possible in order to come up with a plan to help you feel more confident and capable and be as successful as I know you can be in everything you do."

"Okay," I say, because even though I'm scared of what will happen once she sees all the holes and problems and things

89

that are wrong with me, I really like the idea of having a plan to help me not fail.

I follow Dr. Gold across the quiet waiting area to Dr. Sharma's office. Everything is white, like in a hospital. It's not comfortable or cozy at all, but I like Dr. Sharma, too. And not just because I saw a copy of *Harry Potter and the Cursed Child* in the bag next to her desk, but because she talks to me the way Dr. Gold does, like she thinks what I have to say is important.

When Dr. Gold leaves, Dr. Sharma puts a box and a stack of white cards on the table. She takes out a few wooden blocks and asks me questions about them. Then she arranges the rest of the blocks and puts one of the cards in front of me. There's a special design on it. She gives me all kinds of instructions. I listen to what she says and move the blocks around on different cards. I try really hard, and I only second-guess myself once. I keep looking up at Dr. Sharma to see how I'm doing, but she has the world's best poker face, so it's impossible to tell, until I sneak a look at my score sheet. I don't understand everything, but there are a lot of low numbers, like 5 and 7, which I know can only mean one thing: I got a lot of questions wrong.

When I finally get home, I'm so tired. I go up to my room, turn on the thunderstorm, and start my homework. Ms.

Curtis made sure I got all my assignments ahead of time. I've been staring at my math homework for almost an hour when I get a text from Red: How did the test go?

Kind of okay, I answer. *Dr. Gold =* ☺

That's cool. Do you have it?

No idea. I find out on Friday.

Isn't it like a yes or no question?

I guess not, I write back.

I totally don't get ADD.

Me neither, I text. *BTW ADD doesn't exist anymore. You have to call it ADHD now.*

Weird.

I know, right? So, what did I miss in practice?

Everything. We learned a bunch of super advanced opening strategies.

UGH. JEALOUS, I say.

Don't worry. I took notes for you. You're going to be obsessed.

You rock! I text, because it feels good that Red was thinking about me when I wasn't there.

☺. That wasn't even the best part! Mr. Lee finally announced who's coming to chess camp and it's really, really, really good.

Tell me now!

Nope, he writes. Guess.

Don't do this to me, I type as fast as I can.

Hint: Think big.

He's not going to tell me until I give him at least one name. I try to think of who I want it to be—a national, no, a world champion, like Judit Polgar or Magnus Carlsen.

I type **Katerina Nino** and press *send*. She's the youngest national champion ever, and even though she lives in Palo Alto, California, now, she grew up twenty minutes outside of Boston, too.

Ding. Ding. Ding.

"OMG!!!" I scream, even though I'm sitting in my room by myself. **Are you messing with me?** I write. **Because if you are this might actually be the meanest thing you've ever done.**

Red doesn't say anything back. When I pick up my phone to call him, it starts buzzing in my hand, because he's calling me.

"I would never joke about Katerina!" he says as soon as I pick up. "Mr. Lee used to train with her, back in the day."

"Shut up!" I say. "I can't believe this is happening."

"I know, right? I'm really glad I got to tell you, even though I obviously wish you'd been in school today."

"Same."

"BTW, I can't hang out on Friday."

"Really? Why not?" I ask.

"Busy," he says. I keep waiting for him to explain, but he doesn't. It's weird. I can't remember the last time we didn't have movie night. And I was sort of counting on hanging out with Red before the tournament, so we could practice.

"What are you doing?" I ask.

"Dylan invited me to sleep over."

"Oh. Cool," I say, even though I think it's the least cool thing I've ever heard.

I think about telling him to delete our texts, because the last thing I need is for Red to leave his phone out and for Dylan to read all about my personal business. But Red can't know how I feel about Dylan, and I don't want to make it seem like I'm asking him to pick, even though I want him to pick me.

Day two with Dr. Sharma is mostly the same as day one. Only Mom doesn't come inside the office. She drops me off and says good-bye from the car. Instead of moving blocks around on the table, Dr. Sharma reads numbers to me and I have to repeat them back to her, like a monkey. Then she has me look at different lines and shapes. I have to draw exactly what I see or connect a bunch of dots to create circles and squares and other designs.

After we take a break, I read sentences and answer yes-or-no questions that seem to go on forever.

When I'm finally done and home, Dr. Gold calls our house and asks to speak with me. Mom puts the phone on speaker and sits next to me. "One of the things I'm doing as part of my evaluation is speaking with your teachers. Normally I would have this conversation in person, but I was hoping you could tell me a little more about what happened while you were playing human chess at practice the other day."

"Why does that matter?" I ask, because I really don't want to talk about it.

"I want to hear your perspective. That matters more to me than what anyone else says." Dr. Gold sounds serious, like she wants me to know she means it.

"I wasn't trying to ruin the game," I say. "I was mad. I had the answer, and Red wasn't listening to me. He was just following whatever Dylan said, even though we're best friends, not them."

"It sounds like maybe your emotions took over?"

"Pretty much."

"Has that ever happened to you before?" she asks.

I think about saying no, because that's what I want the answer to be, but Dr. Gold is trying to help me and I don't want to make it even harder for her. "It happens a lot."

"Okay," she says softly, like it really is, and I don't need to be embarrassed by that part of myself in front of her, even though I am.

I'm in my room, trying to finish my homework, when my phone buzzes.

We got an A on our lab! ☺ It's Sanam.

Fist bump, I text her.

Go team! she writes back. Science was so boring and way harder without you. Please tell me you're coming back tomorrow.

I think about telling her why I've been out, because I want her to know, but I also don't think it's a very smart idea to tell her over text, so I just write, ☺ *Totes*.

Phew, she writes. See you tomorrow!

SIX.

THE NEXT DAY, I'm excited to see Red and talk about Katerina being at chess camp. Only, when I get to school, Red isn't at our bench. I sit down and wait for him, but after a few minutes, I start to look around, because he's never this late. That's when I realize he's already here, standing on the opposite side of the crowded courtyard with Dylan and the field hockey girls.

Even though seventh grade only started a few weeks ago, I can tell there are all these new, unspoken rules that didn't exist last year, like how out of nowhere being early to hang out before school starts is cool. And how it's totally regular for guys and girls, who aren't best friends like Red and me, to stand next to each other and talk in a group.

I make my way through the crowd and over to Red. It's weird that he's waiting in a new place with a big crew, and I'm walking up to them like I'm the one who doesn't belong. But as soon as Red smiles at me, everything feels good and regular again. "You're back," he says, like he's surprised and maybe he forgot I was only missing two days.

"We were all *so* worried about you," Quinn says.

"Speak for yourself." Dylan looks at Quinn, and then at me. "I didn't notice you were gone. Where were you anyway?"

I can't believe I didn't think about how I was going to answer this question until now. Before I have a chance to respond, Quinn answers for me, "They're trying to figure out what's wrong with her."

"Um, everything," someone says under their breath.

One of the other girls giggles.

My chest tightens. I wish getting made fun of didn't hurt so much every time and I could get better at it, like I have with chess, but it's the kind of thing that never seems to get easier.

"It's too bad you can't play chess anymore," Quinn says.

"I am playing chess!" I shout back.

"Wow," Quinn says. "It's not my fault you're bad at everything."

"I got tested for ADHD," I say. "It's really not a big deal. A lot of people have it." I try to sound confident.

"A lot of smart people, like Albert Einstein and JFK and Mozart," Red adds.

Einstein? Really? I definitely didn't know that.

"Because clearly Clea is just like Einstein." Quinn laughs. "I'm not trying to be mean or anything, but smart people don't get Fs." She looks at me when she says it.

"Don't," Red whispers to me.

But it hurts so much, and before I can take a breath or think or stop myself, the words are out of my mouth, flying through the air, like the letters and sounds and syllables are in control, not me. "I didn't get an F!" I shout. "I didn't!"

Quinn doesn't say anything. No one does. It's silent. Everyone around us stops talking. They stare at me and then at each other, trading silent messages with their eyes, making it obvious that they think Quinn is right about me.

The bell rings, and everyone but Red disappears inside.

Red stays next to me. "Thanks," I say. "For backing me up." Because I want him to know it matters.

"I should have cut you off before—" he says.

I shake my head. "You tried. I'm sorry. I won't do anything like that ever again."

"Okay. Sure," Red says, like he really doesn't believe me.

"I promise," I say.

"I mean, that would be good."

"I didn't know all those people had ADHD," I say.

"Yeah, me neither. I looked it up after we talked, because I realized I didn't actually know anything about it," he says. "I was surprised. Everyone on the list I found was smart or really talented."

"I mean, if smart people have it then I probably don't," I say.

"Maybe you do?"

"I'm scared to find out. I feel like no matter what happens, it's going to be bad."

"It can't really get worse," he says.

I nod, except deep down I'm afraid it's never going to get better, because Quinn is right—I'm stupid. Smart people don't get Fs.

I'm in science, pouring distilled water into a plastic cup, when Sanam whispers in my ear, "Do you like-like Red?"

"Definitely not," I say.

"Really? You're, like, one hundred percent sure?"

"I am. I swear," I say.

"Hmm. I really thought you wanted to be BF-GF with him."

"He doesn't give me that feeling—in my stomach."

She nods. "I get what you mean."

"Who told you I did?" I ask.

"No one. I just wanted to check."

"I mean, I'd obviously tell you if I liked him," I say.

She adds a pinch of baking soda to the cup and says, "Don't tell anyone this, but I, um . . ." She stops herself. "Never mind."

"I won't tell. Cross my heart." I look at her. "I swear—on chess."

Sanam takes a deep breath and then leans in closer. "I think I, um, like-like him. Red, I mean."

"What?!" My voice comes out a little too loud.

The girls at the table in front of us turn around and stare.

"Shhh!" Sanam says.

"I'm sorry. I just—wow. I had no clue." I lower my voice. "But that's cool. I promise not to tell."

"Has he, um, ever said anything about me?" Sanam looks at her hands.

"I mean, he's always talking about how you're way better at chess than he is. It comes up kind of a lot. And I don't think he likes anyone else, because I'm pretty sure he would have told me if he did."

Sanam smiles. "Good to know."

"Fingers crossed he likes you back." I cross my fingers on both hands.

Sanam does, too.

It feels important, like a secret friendship pact.

After lunch, I go straight to chess practice and find my spot on the pairing sheet. I'm playing Quinn.

No! Why me?

I sit down across the table from her without looking up. She's the last person on earth I want to deal with right now. I can't wait to start playing. All I want to do is zone out and float away to a far-off land where I'm not the problem. Except when I look at the board, half the pieces are missing.

"Welcome to Pawn Wars," Mr. Lee says. "There should be two rows of pawns on the board in front of you. The player who gets one of their pawns to the other side first wins. This exercise should help you hone your skills and your pawn strategy. Just as a reminder, this is the last practice before our tournament on Saturday. Please be in our team room at 9:15 a.m. As you know from last year, I like to wait until we're together before I share who will be representing our team. I expect each of you to be on time and ready to play. Also, before you leave today, please sign up to volunteer at the raffle on Monday at lunch. There are a lot of great prizes this year that will help us raise money for our annual chess camp. Any questions before we get started?" I have so many swirling around in my brain, like what are my chances of playing if I don't win right now and how am I supposed to beat Quinn with only pawns. Except I can't ask any of those questions out loud. "Okay, then, get to work," Mr. Lee says.

Quinn hits the clock.

I move my pawn on the queen's side up two squares and then tap the clock.

Quinn slides her pawn on the same file up one spot.

I'm pretty sure I need to get my pawns in a position where they're in little triangles, because I want them to be able to protect each other as I move them forward. I basically need to create a situation where my pawns outnumber Quinn's. That way even if she captures one of mine, I can capture one of hers and still be defended.

At first, my strategy is working really well, except that Quinn has the exact same plan. She moves her pieces quickly and hits the clock in this way, like she thinks she's definitely going to win. And I can't tell if she has experience playing with only pawns, or if she's just acting super confident because that's how she is.

We go head-to-head for a while, until she eventually outnumbers me. I have no idea what I'm supposed to do next. I only have two possible moves and neither one is going to get me to the other side of the board. There's no way for me to win.

I'm about to give up when I realize I only have two legal moves left. If I make both of them and Quinn still hasn't won, it's a draw! It's not winning, but it's a lot better than losing. And if Quinn goes for it, it could maybe be enough to impress Mr. Lee and secure my spot in the tournament.

I slide my pawn up one square.

Quinn immediately captures my pawn with her pawn.

I make the only other legal move I can.

Quinn moves another one of her pawns, toward my side of the board, aiming to win. But there's nothing left for me to do.

I put my hand up so Mr. Lee knows we're done.

"What are you doing?" Quinn glares at me.

"I don't have any moves left," I say. "The game is over."

"Awesome," she says. "I love winning."

"It's a draw," I correct her.

"That's what I meant," she says quickly, trying to pick up the pieces, but it's too late. I already know.

Mr. Lee walks over to us, holding his clipboard. "Great work thinking on your feet, Clea. Very smart strategy." He's looking at the board and nodding, like even though I didn't win, he's still impressed. Like maybe my draw is enough to convince him that I'm advanced and ready to play in the tournament.

SEVEN.

ON FRIDAY, MY stomach is fluttering when Mom and I get to Dr. Gold's office. Dad is in the waiting room. He smiles as soon as we walk in and moves his luggage out of the way to make space for us. He hugs me, squeezing extra tight, and then kisses Mom, wrapping his arm around her. He doesn't let go, even after we all sit down. His hand stays firm against her shoulder.

Dad has been in California all week working on some "big deal" that's going to take up a lot of extra time. For the next few months, he's not always going to be home on Thursdays. It's only been one week and I already hate it. Sometimes I wonder what it would be like to have the kind of dad who stayed in the same place as me all the time. And then I think about Red, and how his dad is never home because he lives in a different state, and I feel bad being upset when he has it so much worse.

Mom whispers something in Dad's ear. I wonder if she's talking softly because she doesn't want me to know what she's saying, or if there's some secret rule that we're not supposed to disturb other people's waiting. We aren't the only ones in the room today. There are a few other families, but it's still silent.

I put in my earbuds and turn on one of my shows, because I want to zone out for a few minutes. Only, Mom keeps glancing over at me when she thinks I'm not looking, like she's checking to make sure I'm okay. And I would be fine, if she'd stop staring and making it impossible for me to think about anything other than what's about to happen when Dr. Gold finally opens the door.

I'm not sure I know how I feel, other than nervous. No matter what she says, the news is going to be bad. I don't want her to say everything is fine, when I know deep down it's not, and I don't want anything to be really wrong with me, either.

Dr. Gold opens the door and says, "Come on in." She's wearing a long dress that's covered with pink and purple flowers. I walk into her office first and pick the chair by the door. Mom and Dad sit next to each other on the sofa.

"Welcome," she says to Dad. "And welcome back." She smiles at Mom and then at me.

It feels hot and cramped in her office today with an extra person. Everything seems smaller. I look down at the shaggy rug and remind myself to breathe.

Dr. Gold continues. "Let me start by saying that you did very well on the intelligence test, Clea."

I look up at her, because I'm not sure I heard her correctly.

"That's good, right?" Mom's words rattle together.

Dr. Gold nods.

"No way," I say. "That's definitely a mistake."

"It's not, Clea," Dr. Gold says. "You have a high IQ. And you don't have a learning disability that might be causing additional processing challenges."

"So what's wrong with me?" I blurt out.

"I know you're eager for an answer, and you will have one very soon. But what I want to do right now is share what Ms. Curtis and I both observed during your evaluation, as well as some of the challenges that your teachers shared with

107

Ms. Curtis. Then we can talk about the root of those challenges. Does that sound okay to you?"

"Um, I guess," I say, because I don't want to be rude. But I really wish she'd get it over with and tell us already.

Dr. Gold looks at her notes. "We noticed that you struggle to follow instructions. You have a hard time listening, and paying close attention to details is difficult. You're easily distracted during class and at home, and forgetful when it comes to things you're expected to do every day. It's hard for you to stay focused. These are all symptoms of inattention," she says. "At the same time, you also struggle with impulsivity. It can be challenging for you to wait your turn and take your time, which can cause you to fall and run into things. You have a tendency to blurt out what you're thinking, interrupt conversations, and talk over people."

"I still don't get it," I say. "Nothing you said is that a big of a deal."

"I was just thinking that," Dad agrees. "All of those things happen to me."

"The difference is Clea experiences these symptoms persistently. They're enduring and constant for her. And while each one on its own might not seem like a big deal, when you put them together and they're happening at the same time, they can get in the way and create a lot of problems. They already have."

"Oh. Okay," Dad says. "I can see that."

Mom nods. "Me too."

"The official diagnosis is attention-deficit/hyperactivity disorder: predominantly inattentive presentation."

"I don't get what having ADHD means," I say. "Like, what's going to happen to me now?"

"That's a great question," Dr. Gold says. "Ms. Curtis and I will work together and come up with a plan to support you in school, which will include things like organizational help, weekly check-ins, and extra time. Then I'll speak with your parents about the possibility of combining our plan with medication to help with your symptoms."

"So, basically this is, like, a fancy medical way of saying I'm stupid and lazy and here's a pill to fix everything, right?"

"ADHD has nothing to do with intelligence or work ethic." Dr. Gold looks right at me when she says it.

"That makes no sense," I say. "I need to try harder and focus so I stop messing everything up."

Dr. Gold takes a deep breath. "Clea, because you are so capable, intelligent, and driven to succeed, you have been able to compensate for your ADHD, but as the demands of school have increased, managing your work has become more challenging. I suspect that has created confusion about what it means to work hard, and that you've spent a lot of time blaming yourself for not putting in enough effort or for not being good enough, because you didn't realize that ADHD was standing in your way."

All the things Dr. Gold just said seem like they could be true, but it still feels like everything that's been happening in school is my fault, even if I have ADHD. Now I'm afraid that maybe I messed up her test, too, because that's kind of my thing lately. I don't want her to give me a plan or a pill that doesn't work because she thinks I'm something I'm not.

"I don't think I should take medicine," I say.

"Clea," Mom says. "That's a decision for the adults."

I can't let Mom, Dad, and Dr. Gold sit around talking about me when I'm not in the room. And I don't want my parents to decide. They never know what's right for me anymore, like with chess and how they want me to quit even though I love it. "It's happening to me. I should get a say."

"I know, sweetheart, but this is a very serious decision. Dad and I will figure out what's best for you."

"I bet." I roll my eyes. "Because you're so good at that."

"Don't be rude," Dad says.

"I'm being honest," I say. "I don't want to take medicine."

"I'm sorry you feel that way," Mom says. "But if there is a way to solve this problem, we're going to at least consider the option."

"And I'm sorry—for being such a huge problem," I say back.

"That's not what I meant, and you know it."

Only I don't.

"I like to be transparent with my patients at every age, especially when they ask to be involved," Dr. Gold says. "What might work best is if we all discuss the option of medication now, take the weekend to digest, and come back together next week to make a decision. And if your parents have follow-up questions, I can find a separate time to talk with them, since ultimately they will be the ones deciding if medicine is or isn't right for you."

"That works for me," Dad says.

"Me too," Mom says.

"Fine," I say, because I like that Dr. Gold always talks to me. And even though I don't think it's fair that what happens is 100 percent up to my parents, I know nothing I say is going to change the fact that they're adults and I'm not.

"Okay, good," Dr. Gold says. "First of all, I want to be clear that ADHD is a variation of how some people's attention systems work. It's something you'll have to learn to manage, but nothing is broken. So the medication used to treat ADHD is not a 'problem solver.'" Dr. Gold looks at Mom. "That said, we have found that when medicine is prescribed in conjunction with educational support, patients have a very high rate of success managing their symptoms. If you are open to a combination treatment plan, I'd recommend a very low-dose stimulant, which would increase dopamine levels in Clea's brain to boost concentration and reduce impulsivity. The medication I'd likely prescribe would take about twenty minutes to an hour to kick in, and it would work for about twelve hours."

"Are there side effects?" Dad asks.

"Short term there can be reduced appetite, agitation, stomachaches, and trouble sleeping. We'd want to monitor Clea closely to make sure we have the right medication and the correct dose, especially as she continues to grow. But there are no major long-term effects."

"How could anyone know that?" Dad asks. "These medications are so new."

"That's actually not true. The main ingredients in the

stimulant I'd likely prescribe are amphetamine, which was first synthesized in 1887, and methylphenidate, developed in 1944," Dr. Gold explains. "A lot of research has been done on both."

"Interesting," Mom says.

"I don't know." Dad shakes his head.

"I would encourage you to hold off on making any decisions right now. Give yourself time to think through this information over the weekend and take home some reading material." Dr. Gold picks pamphlets off her desk and hands one to each of us. "There will be some trial and error. And whatever plan you decide on doesn't have to be forever. The goal is to figure out what Clea needs to manage her ADHD. You can always commit to one approach and then reevaluate if the plan isn't working."

"That makes sense," Dad says.

"How long does the trial-and-error part take?" I ask, because even though I don't want to try medicine, I really *do* need things to get better in school.

"It's different for everyone," Dr. Gold says. "The plan we come up with first could help right away—"

"That would be great," I say.

"It would be," Dr. Gold says. "It might also take a little

113

time to figure out exactly what you need. But if you are open to the options and willing to work with Ms. Curtis and with me, we will find a plan that makes school much more manageable for you."

Even though I'm scared, I know Dr. Gold wants to help me and I need to try as hard as I can to trust her. "Okay," I say. "I am."

"Good," Dr. Gold says. "We'll start implementing an education plan right away. That will help you a lot. And we can talk more about medicine next week."

"It would have to be Monday morning," Dad says. "I leave for the airport at ten."

Dr. Gold picks up her phone and scrolls through her schedule. "Does seven thirty work?"

Mom and Dad both nod.

She types something and then says, "Okay, well, then I'll—"

"Wait," I shout, before she can end our session. Everyone looks at me. "Remember before when you said my intelligence test was good. Are you sure? Can you check my answers one more time?" I ask, because the test is the reason Dr. Gold thinks I'm smart, which means the results have to be wrong.

"Dr. Sharma is extremely thorough, so I'm very confident

that the score is right," Dr. Gold says. "Clea, I think it's important for you to hear that ADHD and intelligence are not connected. They're completely separate. When you can concentrate and you aren't distracted, your brain is very capable."

I nod, because I can see what she's saying, and I want to believe her.

When our appointment is over, Mom rushes out of Dr. Gold's office, because she needs to pick Henley up from speech therapy.

By the time Dad and I get outside, she's already gone.

We walk over to the car, and as soon as I get in and close the door, Dad turns on Kiss 108, because he knows it's my favorite station.

"How was California?" I ask before he has a chance to question me about ADHD or medication or anything else.

"Not as good as home. I always miss my girls." I already know Dad doesn't like being away for work, but it feels good to hear him say that we're the reason. It's the kind of thing that never gets old, like plain cheese pizza. It makes me think that maybe I'm not the only one who gets an empty pit in my stomach when he leaves.

"What did you have to do this time?" I roll down the window a little and breathe in the fresh air as we drive home.

"I spent the last few days meeting with people who run different parts of the company we're thinking about buying, and then this morning I toured the factory. Now I have to review the information and the numbers—do some math—and figure out what else I need to know in order to decide if it makes sense for my company to buy this company."

"That sounds really boring," I say. "I mean, no offense."

He smiles. "I think you'd like my job. It's a big puzzle. I have to figure out if the pieces fit together."

"But you have to do math," I say. "Ick."

"That part is easy."

"Not for me."

"I know school has been hard for you, but you're a lot better with numbers than you think you are." Dad's voice is steady, like he really believes what he's saying. I try to let his words sink in, because maybe if I think I'm good at algebra, I will be. It can't hurt. "I can help you with your math home-work this weekend."

"Tonight? After dinner?" I know I need to schedule a time if I want it to happen, which I do, since Dad is the best at explaining math to me in a way I can actually understand.

"Isn't Red coming over?" he asks.

I shake my head.

"Is everything okay?"

"Yeah. It's fine," I lie.

"Let's go over your math problems tomorrow," he says. "I have some work I need to finish up tonight."

"We'll be home from the tournament after lunch," I say. "Mr. Lee said I might get picked to play, because I'm really good."

"That's great, kiddo," Dad says. "I have a few calls in the early afternoon, but we'll find a time. Sunday might be better."

I nod and try not to get my hopes up too high, because this is what always happens. Dad wants to help me, but then he can't because of work or Henley or something else that needs him more than I do.

When we pull into the driveway, Red is on our back steps, like we're supposed to hang out.

"I called you a million times. Why didn't you check your phone?" His voice sounds shrill and his eyes look sad.

"What's wrong?" I ask.

"My dad was sitting in the kitchen when Edie and I got home from school. He expects us to drop everything and go to some stupid lake in New Hampshire with him and Barf.

I mean, we have a tourney tomorrow. And I'm never going anywhere with her." Red's voice is loud. "I want her to stay in Colorado where she belongs. I hate her face. It looks like it's made out of plastic. And she's always smirking, like she's so happy about ruining my life." He looks right at me with his dark blue eyes. I've never seen him like this—angry and loud, like he's about to explode.

I wish I knew what to do or say to make it better for him, but I can't think of anything. He doesn't look away. He stares at me, like he wants what I want—for me to be able to fix his family. "I'm so sorry," I say. I sit down next to him on the steps, even though there's barely enough room for both of us.

"Everyone kept telling me to calm down—even my mom. And now I feel like maybe they're right and I totally overreacted."

"No way. You didn't do anything wrong," I say firmly, because I know I'm right. "Your dad is the one who messed up by moving away and flaking on you, and he can't just expect you to go on a last-minute trip with him and his barf-y girlfriend. So, no, you don't have to be calm if you don't feel like it."

Red nods, like he's trying hard to believe me. He takes a deep breath and lets out all the air in one big, long sigh, like he's deflating, and then leans forward and puts his head in his hands. I don't notice right away, but his back is pulsing, and every few seconds he rubs his eyes. I'm pretty sure he's crying. I've only ever seen Red cry one other time, when he got hit in the leg with a baseball during gym, but that was a different kind of crying. He was hurt on the outside, and after the bruise healed, we never talked about it again, because it didn't matter. Not like this.

I put my hand on his shoulder, and then I don't know what to do with it. If Henley were upset, I'd rub her back and tell her it was going to be okay, but this doesn't feel the same, and not just because this situation probably won't be okay for a long time, maybe forever. Something about rubbing Red's back feels awkward now that my hand is there. Only before I can move away, he leans into me, like he's so tired he can't hold himself up anymore. His head is heavy against my shoulder. I leave my hand where it is on his fleecy jacket, because I want him to stay next to me, until he feels better.

When he finally sits up, his eyes are red and swollen. He looks down at his phone. "Edie is picking me up soon," he says. "She needs to drive me to Dylan's now, because she's sleeping over at a friend's house tonight, too."

I ignore the sleepover comment. I don't want to think

about the fact that Red is leaving to hang out with Dylan instead of staying to eat pizza and watch movies with me.

"What does Edie think about everything?" I ask.

"She acts like it's not happening, which isn't fair at all. I mean, she's the only one who gets what it feels like to have our dad move across the country and, you know, not be around and stuff. We're going through the same thing. But it's almost like we're not. Ugh, I'm sick of talking about my stupid family."

"I know," I say.

"It feels like it's never going to get better."

"I'm sorry." I want to tell him it will, but I'm not sure if that's true and I don't want to lie.

"Wait—where were you before?" he asks. "Why didn't you answer your phone?"

"I was at the doctor," I say.

"Oh yeah. I forgot that was happening today," he says. "So, do you have ADHD?"

"Yes," I say, picking at my nails.

"But do you think you really have it?"

"I have it." I say it like it's a fact, because Dr. Gold said it was. "There are three different kinds. One where you jump out of your seat a lot, and one where you can't pay attention because your brain is being distracted, like, every three seconds. I have that one. And the third kind is where you have the first and second type at the same time. Dr. Gold said once we have a plan and I can concentrate, I'll be good at school again."

"Cool," Red says. "I mean, a plan sounds good. If school weren't so hard, it would be way better."

"Yeah," I say. "It will be."

EIGHT.

THE NEXT MORNING, Henley opens the door to my bedroom, puts her finger up to her mouth, and tiptoes across my room. "Be quiet," she whispers to Hilda.

I keep my eyes mostly closed, because I don't want her to know that I'm already awake. I have been for about ten minutes, ever since she stomped up the stairs, stood on the other side of my bedroom door, and started telling Hilda about her plan to sneak into my room and leave me a surprise that she made for me in school yesterday when they learned about origami.

Henley puts the gift on my bedside table and scampers away, forgetting to close the door behind her. I pull myself out of bed and look to see what she left me. It's a paper fortune-teller. I pick it up and slip my fingers into the pockets. There are four sides and each one is a different color— purple, pink, blue, and green. I pick blue and pull the corners apart. There are numbers inside—one through eight. I choose five, open the tab, and read the message written in Henley's slanted pink handwriting: *You are going to win today!* There are hearts and stars and exclamation points.

I can't help but smile.

I start over. This time I pick purple and the number three. I open the flap and read the message: *You are going to win today!*

I pull open all the flaps. It says the same thing eight times. And even though I know Henley made the fortune-teller for me, it feels like magic that there's a person in the world who thinks I'm definitely going to win, no matter what, just because I'm me.

My phone starts buzzing, but I can't find it. It's not in any of the places I usually put it, so I follow the rumbling over to my dresser. Only it's not there, either. I stand still and listen for the buzzing to start again. The sound is muffled, but I know I'm close. I open the top drawer and rummage around the socks and T-shirts until I find it all the way in the back. It's Red: *Ready to win?*

Don't jinx me, I write back.

Impossible. What are you thinking?

I'm scared to play and more scared not to play. Are you okay? What ended up happening with your dad?

Don't change the subject, he texts. That seems right to me. Your first tournament is a big deal. But you're going to be great. I know it.

Thanks, I tell him.

See you soon .

I only have an hour before the match, and even though I should start my homework, I don't want to. I push my backpack farther into the closet and shut the door, trying to block out everything I have to do after chess. I sit on the carpet and take a deep breath. I need to stay focused and positive if I want to win, and I do more than anything, but I keep wondering if I'm even going to get a chance to play. I try to pretend that it's already been decided, but the information won't stick. Maybe I should do my Spanish homework. I could get it over with quickly, and then I'd feel better about everything else. Or worse. That could happen. I don't know. I could bring my bag to the tournament and try to do some work while I'm at school if I don't get picked. There's no way Mr. Lee is going to choose me. I missed practice. I know he said it didn't matter, and he wouldn't hold it against me, but I'm not *that* good. I mean, I'm better than I was last year and I keep performing in practice. That must mean something. But I'm not Red or Sanam or someone the team actually needs to win the tournament. How could I be? I've never played in one before. I guess maybe I could be. Red thinks I am. And deep down I sort of think I am, too.

I can't find my phone again. I retrace my steps—dresser, closet, and then floor. It has to be here, because I just had it in my hand, and I haven't left my room. I don't remember putting it down, which is not a good sign. I need to settle down, because if I do get picked, I want to be ready to play my best. I spot my phone on the rug under the dresser. But I can't stop wondering what's going to happen. So I take out my computer and open up my chess tactics. I press *start*, and I can feel myself zone in on what I need to do to win. I'm free. And out of my head and my real life. It feels so good, like I'm somewhere else. I never want to stop, but after way too many rounds, I know I need to pull myself away or I'm going to be late, because I still need to shower, get dressed, and eat. Only, I can't look away. I just want to solve one more problem. I press *start*. I can't help it. No. I need to stop. I shut my computer as fast as I can, put it away in my desk where I can't see it. Then I walk out of my room and into the bathroom to shower.

I'm still thinking about how badly I want to play one more round when I walk back into my room, but I don't let myself go anywhere near my desk. I open my dresser, take out my chess team jersey, and pull it over my head. It's green with yellow writing, because those are our school colors. I glance at myself in the mirror. It looks good. The bright green makes my eyes pop the way makeup should, but never does. I look smarter. Okay, I know that's not really possible, but I swear I do, at least I do to me. I look official and ready, like a real chess player, who could maybe even play in a tournament and win.

Mom, Dad, and Henley all drive me to school and walk me inside. I'm so excited that I have to stop myself from sprinting ahead of my family. There are people I've never seen standing in the parking lot and near the entrance to school. I don't want to look unsophisticated or like I'm a flailing mess. First impressions are important, especially in chess. I want everyone to know I'm a serious competitor and a future Master.

There are a lot of people I don't recognize in the hallway leading to the cafeteria—parents, players, and coaches with clipboards—and it's louder in here today than I remember it being last year. I wonder if that's because I'm nervous, since I actually have a chance to play.

I glance into the cafeteria. There are long empty rows of tables with chessboards. My heart speeds up, beating faster and faster inside my chest.

Everywhere I turn I see different team jerseys—red and royal blue and purple. But no one is wearing green and yellow like me. That's when I remember I'm supposed to go straight to the team room. Families aren't allowed in the playing or team rooms during the tournament, because of distractions and also because sometimes parents fight about the results, so even though I probably won't see Mom, Dad, or Henley again until it's all over, or maybe between rounds, it feels good to know they're here. "I have to go meet everyone," I say.

Mom smiles. "We'll be cheering for you!"

"Good luck," Dad says. "Come find us if you need anything."

Henley grabs on to my hand. "Win," she says, like she's putting a spell on me.

"Thank you," I say, looking at all of them.

I take a deep breath and walk to the end of the hall and into our team room, which is actually the lower school music room. There's a keyboard and xylophones in the front, triangles hanging from the ceiling, and no chairs. Mr. Lee is standing by the keyboard when I walk in, staring at his clipboard. He's wearing his chess team jersey, like the rest of us. The material is thick, so there's no way to tell what his secret T-shirt says today. Everyone else is either sitting on the floor or huddled in small groups.

Sanam isn't here yet and neither is Red, which is especially weird, because Dylan is here. I'm about to get my phone out to see if Red texted me when Sanam walks in, drops her bag and coat, and stands next to me. "Nervous?" she asks, twirling the end of her short black hair.

"Uh, yeah," I say.

"I hate waiting to find out. I feel like I'm going to puke."

"You're definitely playing," I say.

"I don't think so." She shakes her head. "I only won one game." She lowers her voice, like she doesn't want anyone else to hear our conversation. I get that losing isn't fun, but if I were smart and one of the best players on our team, like Sanam, I would never be embarrassed about losing one or two games. It's not like a reminder that there's something wrong with her, like it is for me.

"You're so good," I say. "There's no way you're not getting picked."

128

"There's no way *you're* not getting picked," she says.

"I really hope you're right."

"I am."

Mr. Lee claps his hands together, and everyone gathers around him. "These are some of the most determined teams we'll compete against all year. I want you to stay positive for one another throughout the entire tournament."

It's hard for me to concentrate on what he's saying, because people keep walking by the door, and I can't help but look to see if any of them are Red.

"Chess may sometimes feel like an individual game, but it's not. We're a team," Mr. Lee says. "The only way to win is if we work together, those who are playing today and those who aren't. Whether it's your first tournament or your twentieth, competing on this level is challenging." His eyes wander around the circle, landing on each of us. I wonder if he's noticed that Red is missing. "In some ways it gets easier, and in other ways, it's always hard. I hope you will all be encouraging and supportive of one another throughout the day."

I glance at the door again. It's still not Red. I'm starting to worry that maybe his mom made him go to New Hampshire. Now I wish I'd checked my phone.

"Twelve of you will be representing our team today. You've each played very well over the last few weeks and proved that you're ready to compete." Mr. Lee looks at his notes.

I take a deep breath. I really hope my name is on the list. It has to be.

"Mateo and Lily," Mr. Lee says, then looks at each of them before his eyes drop back down into his notebook. "Quinn, Ajay, and Pari." He scans the group. Quinn smiles, looking around at everyone, like she wants to make sure the whole team heard her name called. That's five of the twelve spots. *Breathe. There are still seven left.* "Layla, Ethan, and Red," Mr. Lee says. *Okay, now, four. But it's fine. Don't freak out yet.* "Has anyone seen Red?" Mr. Lee asks. His eyes sweep across the room, and then weave back around in search of him. I think there's someone by the door. But the person keeps walking. It's not him.

Sanam and a few other people look at me.

Only, I don't have the answer.

"I don't think he's coming," Dylan says, like maybe he knows something I don't. I wish it didn't bother me, but it does.

"Okay." Mr. Lee drags out the word and shakes his head, so we know it's actually not okay at all. "Moving on," he says.

130

"Ella and Isaac." Now there are only two spots left and he still hasn't called Dylan or Sanam, which is really not great, since they both have a lot of experience playing in tournaments, and if I were Mr. Lee, I'd definitely pick either of them over me, especially now that Red isn't here. "Dylan."

"Score." Dylan fist-bumps Isaac.

"And last but not least—Clea." He says my name so fast I almost miss it. Except he's looking right at me, so I know it's real. He picked me! I'm playing in the tournament! "And since Red isn't here, let's go ahead and have Harrison sub in for him."

"You're playing!" Sanam shrieks. Her voice sounds happy, but she's staring at the floor, like her head is so heavy she can barely hold it up.

"Are you okay?" I whisper.

She wipes her eyes on her jersey, and I can see how disappointed she is that she's not playing. "I'm really happy for you." She looks up at me, like she wants me to know she means it.

"Thanks," I say, because it feels good to have her on my side.

"Hands in," Mr. Lee says. I follow everyone else's lead and put my hand in the middle of the circle. "Win on three," he says. "One, two, three . . ."

"Win!" everyone shouts at the exact same time. I feel chills up and down my arms, and adrenaline pumping through me.

Mr. Lee makes a few announcements about what we're supposed to do between games. We're divided into quads for this tournament, which means I'll play three rounds of chess today. When Mr. Lee is done explaining everything, I rush over to my bag and pull out my phone as fast as I can to find out what's going on with Red. Only, I don't have any messages from him. No missed calls or voice mails or texts. Nothing.

Are you okay? I write to him. I stare at my phone, willing him to write back before someone notices I'm standing here, instead of checking the pairing list and taking my seat. When I look up again, most of the team has cleared out of the room. I'm alone, and he still hasn't written back. I put my phone on vibrate, slip it into my pocket, even though it's against the rules, and sprint down the hall to find my name. I'm playing black and my opponent is someone named Ruby Jacobson.

Most people are already in their seats by the time I walk into the cafeteria and look around the room for my board. Even though technically no one is talking, it's even louder in here than it was in the hall. Every whisper and sigh echoes off the walls, bouncing around the room and back at me. When I spot my board in the middle of the center table, I walk over, shake Ruby's hand, and sit down across from her. She has wide eyes, long red hair in a French braid, and a freckly face. I really wish the copper streaks didn't remind me of Red, and the fact that I still haven't felt my phone vibrate.

There are people on all sides of me, and the boards feel cramped even closer together today than during practice, even though I don't think they are. I can feel my shoulders scrunch together, like I'm trying to make myself smaller so that I have more space and air and quiet to myself. Only, it doesn't help. There's a heavy breather on my left, and the girl on my right sounds like a cow chomping down on too many pieces of cinnamon gum. The strong smell makes me queasy. I don't know if it's because the room is bigger or because there are more people than I'm used to, but I can't turn off all the noises— pencils and fingernails tapping and scratching. I'm suffocating on other people's sounds.

I take a deep breath and remind myself that Mr. Lee picked me to represent our team. I can't let everyone down. I visualize my pawns keeping each other safe, so that hopefully in the endgame they can get promoted and help me win my first round. I can do this. I open my chess notebook and pick up my pencil. *Move. Let go. Tap. Write.* I sing the words over in my head.

I tap the clock and Ruby makes her first move.

I slide one of my pawns out, responding to Ruby. We go back and forth a few times, and I can tell right away that she's good. Not better than me on my best day, but today doesn't feel like that. I'm not in the zone. I glance away from the board so many times, which I never do. I try to concentrate for long enough to chart my next few steps, but the girl with the gum is slurping and swallowing and gnawing, and I'm pretty sure my phone is buzzing in my pocket. I don't let myself look away from the board. I move my rook over and capture the enemy queen. But I can't stop worrying about Red.

Ruby takes out my bishop with hers, giving her direct access to my king.

I slide my king over one square, tap the clock, write down both of our moves, and look back up as fast as I can, because I need to know what she does next.

There are adults on the other side of the doors that separate the cafeteria and the hallway, "whispering" and setting up snacks, like they don't realize we're all in here trying to play chess. Mr. Lee walks over to them holding his finger up to his mouth, and they immediately stop talking, but it reminds me how many other noises there are and how distracted I am.

I look back down at the board, because I need to focus on

what's happening in front of me. It's the only way I'm going to win.

Ruby moves her pawn up one square, smiles with her eyes, and taps the clock.

My king is in danger. I just need to find a place to move. Only every square is taken by one of my pieces or under direct attack by one of her bishops.

"Checkmate," Ruby says.

It's over. Just like that. She's won.

When I look up, Ruby is already standing with her hand out. "Good game."

"Good game," I say, but my words barely make it out. I lost. I don't understand why I couldn't get in the zone.

I hide out in the bathroom between rounds, because I don't want to see Quinn or Dylan or anyone else who will make me feel even worse than I already do. I lock the door and take my phone out of my pocket to look at Red's message, except there isn't one. He still hasn't written back.

I want to tell him that I lost my first tournament game, because he'll know exactly what to say to make me feel better. But I don't, because he's not here, and it seems like wherever he is he doesn't have his phone, and I'm starting to get the sense that something is really, really wrong.

I hope you're okay, I text.

My phone buzzes back right away. *I'm here,* he writes.

I rush out of the bathroom, into the team room, and over to Red. "What happened?" I ask.

"Nothing," he says. "I was late."

"I know, but I mean, are you okay?"

"Yeah. I'm fine." He sounds annoyed.

"You don't seem fine," I say.

"Stop. I don't want to talk to you." He gives me a look I've never seen before, like he doesn't get what my problem is or why I'm standing here.

"Dude," Dylan shouts, walking over to us. "You're here. Everything cool?"

"It's all good, bro," Red says. "I'm just annoyed I can't forget the drama and crush some people in chess."

"For real," Dylan says, and they high-five.

My cheeks are burning and probably red by now, so it's obvious that I'm hurt, because I get that something happened and he told Dylan, not me, even though we're best friends who tell each other everything. And it's not okay, but I don't say that, because it kind of has to be.

I run my fingers through my hair, which is still wet and a little sticky in the back like I didn't wash it. Only, I did.

Something about the way it feels makes me itchy and uncomfortable. I want to take another shower and start this whole day over.

After the break, I check the pairing list and head back to the middle of the cafeteria for round two. I'm basically in the same seat as last time, only on the other side of the long table and over one board. I'm playing white this round. I stare at the pieces, thinking through my strategy and trying to find my way into the chess tunnel, where it's safe and noise-free, before my new opponent, Amir, and everyone else takes their seats.

I keep thinking that my phone is humming against my leg and that maybe it's Red apologizing or explaining what happened. He didn't even ask if I got picked to play. But when I slide my phone out of my pocket and turn on the screen to check, there are no new messages.

A tall cute boy with brown hair and skin sits down across from me. His eyes stay glued to the board between us, and I'm so jealous of how focused he looks, I could scream. I cover my mouth with both hands to make sure that doesn't happen.

I spend the entire match looking around the room, down at my pencil, at the tag on my shirt that's rubbing against my skin, and at the boy next to me who keeps chewing nervously on the inside of his cheek and cracking his knuckles.

Amir only glances away from the board once—the first time he taps the clock to start the match. It only takes him twenty moves to beat me, which is embarrassing.

I don't know what's happening to me, but I need to do something fast. I only have one more round to prove that I'm not a total flop.

I walk as fast as I can out of the cafeteria without drawing attention to myself and try my best to disappear into the crowded hall, heading straight for the door, because I need fresh air or a change of scenery or something to help me concentrate.

"Clea," Sanam says, stopping me by the apple cider. "How's it going?"

"Okay," I say, then keep walking until I'm outside, where it's cool and quiet and there's space to think. I sit down on one of the benches in front of the building, close my eyes, and breathe.

When I open them again, Sanam is standing in front of me, holding two paper cups. "I didn't believe you." She hands me a cider and sits down.

"Thanks." I take a sip of the warm juice.

"You're welcome." She doesn't say anything else. We're both quiet for a few minutes. And even though everything feels hard right now, it's nice not to be alone.

"I lost," I say. "Twice. I can't win."

"You have to." She looks right at me. "We're counting on you."

"It's too late." I shake my head.

"It's not. Seriously. Every round is important. You still have another chance. This game could be the difference between winning the tournament and not. Mr. Lee was probably only counting on you to win one game anyway. It's your first tournament. So, one out of three would be totally respectable. I swear"—she pauses—"on the championship."

I nod, because I know how serious Sanam is about our team being the best. "I keep messing up, because I'm—" I stop myself. This can't be happening. It's that thing Dr. Gold was talking about where my brain keeps getting interrupted. "This has never ever happened to me during chess." Chess isn't like everything else.

"Tournaments are different than practice. It's a lot harder to concentrate."

If Sanam has a hard time focusing during tournaments, I don't have a chance. "What do you do?" I ask.

"I try to remind myself to look at the whole board, even if all the action is happening in one area. Before I take my turn, I zoom out for a second and make sure I'm not missing a sneak attack or an opportunity. It's easy to forget the big picture and lose focus when there are so many things happening in the room."

"Yeah. Seriously," I say. "I'm pretty sure I can do that."

"You can. Mr. Lee wouldn't have picked you if he didn't think you could win. You're good, and I'm not saying that because we're friends. Just go back in there and play your best."

"Okay." I know she's right. I can win.

We still have a little time before the final round. I find Mom, Dad, and Henley by the donuts. "You got picked!" Henley shouts as soon as she sees me.

"I did." I put my arm around her.

"This is very exciting," Dad says.

"Thanks," I say.

"Did you win?" Henley looks up at me. "The fortune-teller said so."

"Not yet. But I will." I try to sound sure of myself.

"Because you're the best at chess!" she says.

I pull Henley in close and hold on tight, hoping a little of

140

her confidence will rub off on me before it's time to play again.

I don't want to feel rushed going into the next game, so I walk back into the cafeteria and find my seat in the middle of the room—again. There's only one other person at the long table when I get there: Dylan. He's next to me. I accidentally make eye contact with him when I sit down, and then look away as fast as I can, because I need to concentrate. I can't afford to be distracted by him or Red or anything else. Only, he's making that impossible, because I can feel him staring at me.

We aren't supposed to talk in the cafeteria at all, but most of the seats are empty, and all the coaches are on the other side of the room. So I turn my head to look at Dylan, because I want to get this over with and focus on winning my last game.

"What?" I ask.

He pushes his hair out of his eyes and then does it again, like he's nervous and isn't sure what to do with his hands. "I feel really bad for Red." His voice is soft and serious, like he's trying to actually talk to me. "I can't believe it, you know? I didn't think things could get worse."

"Yeah." I nod and act like I know exactly what's going on,

141

because I don't want to admit that I have no clue what he's talking about or think about the fact that Red doesn't want to talk to me about whatever it is.

"It's like no one even cares about him. His dad is all like 'Barb and I got married and we're having a baby, so she's in your family now. Deal with it.'"

WHAT?! My stomach clenches. It feels like I just got kicked in the gut, and there are so many questions spinning and swirling around in my brain. *How could his dad get married without telling them? Why didn't he invite them? Didn't he want them there? They're having a baby?*

"You didn't know," Dylan says.

I think about denying it. I don't need Dylan to rub it in that Red told him and not me and make me feel even worse. But I'm still in shock, and before I have a chance to say or do anything, he says, "Please don't tell him I told you. I swear I thought you knew." His voice is shaky, like maybe keeping Red's secret actually matters to him, which is weird, because until right now I didn't realize anything mattered to Dylan.

"You can't tell anyone else," I say.

"I won't. I haven't," he says right back. "I promise."

"You better not be lying," I say.

"I swear. He told me last night, and you're seriously the only person I've talked to since then, other than him." *Why didn't Red tell me what happened? Why would he pick Dylan?* "You believe me, right?"

"Yeah," I say quietly, because I guess I do. I bite down on the inside of my mouth and then look at the board in front of me. I take a deep breath and try to find my way into the tunnel. I still have a chance to make a comeback. Sanam said so. Right now I need to forget about Red and Dylan and win my match.

A few minutes later, my new opponent, Regan, is sitting across from me. I glance up right before we start playing, and then I don't look away again for the entire game. I follow Sanam's advice and remind myself to scan the whole board every time it's my turn to make a move. *Zoom out. Move. Let go. Tap. Write.*

Only it doesn't matter that my eyes are laser focused, because my thoughts are pinging from Red to the baby to all the things I could have done to make him not want to tell me . . . then back to the board. I'm trying so hard to concentrate, but before I realize what's happening—ping—I'm on to the next thing. It's like my brain is on scan, shuffling through radio stations, and there's no way to press *stop*. No matter what I do, I can't get my mind to stay in one place, on one track—on chess.

I don't have time to think ahead or come up with a plan for my pieces, and without a strategy, there's no way I can win.

When the third round is finally over, and I've officially lost all three games, the adrenaline pumping through me starts to evaporate. My eyes are heavy. I'm having a hard time keeping them open. I can't stop yawning. I could fall asleep standing up on my walk from the cafeteria to the team room, which is all happy and hopeful and makes everything worse.

I hand my notations to Mr. Lee.

He glances down at the answer key to see what happened, and then back at me. His forehead wrinkles up, like a ruffled potato chip, and I can tell he's sorry I lost and maybe sorry that he let me play. I want to apologize for being so bad, but I'm afraid if I say anything I'll start to cry, and I can't—not in front of the team. I've already embarrassed myself enough for one day. I was the wrong choice. It should have been Sanam or anyone else. I'm not as good as he thinks—not at chess or anything important. I stare at the floor and walk straight to the back of the room, wishing I could vanish into the air. I'm sick of disappointing people.

I plant myself in the back corner and try to hide. Quinn walks right over and sits down. "Win or lose?" Her voice cuts into me. She's waiting for my answer, like where we stand is all up to me, and I guess that's because it's up to everyone playing to win, and I lost. I had a chance to help our team, and I let everyone down.

I take a deep breath. "Lose," I say as fast as I can.

"Seriously? You didn't win one round?"

I shake my head.

She rolls her eyes. "I knew you were bad, but—no one loses all three games. That's not a thing that happens on this team. I don't know if you heard, but we're actually good. Or we used to be, before Red started showing up late and Mr. Lee started picking charity cases."

I don't say anything else. I don't want to make excuses.

We lose the tournament, and I'm pretty sure it's mostly because of me.

Mom, Dad, and Henley are waiting in the lobby by the entrance.

"Clea!" Henley runs over. "You did your *towrn-ament*! Was it fun?"

I look behind me to make sure no one from the team is standing there, and then I turn back around and force myself to smile for my sister. I want her to know hard work pays off and fortunes are real and anything is possible, because those things are true for her, even if they aren't for me. "You know it!" My voice sounds a little too happy. I hope she can't tell.

"Yes!" she says, rushing to keep up with me. "I knew it."

I push open the door to the building and walk outside. Luckily we parked right in front of school, so we don't have to walk too far to get away.

"Clea, honey, we're so proud of you for giving it your all and trying your best." Mom rubs my shoulder.

I want to scream at her that today was the exact opposite of my best, but I bite down on my lip as hard as I can, because I don't want to freak out in front of Henley.

Only I keep thinking about what Sanam said—that tournaments are different than practice. It's a lot harder to concentrate in a big room with all the people and pressure, even for someone without ADHD. Out of nowhere, I'm afraid that it doesn't matter how well I can play in practice or that I've

146

always been able to get in the zone during chess. Maybe tournaments are like tests, and no matter how hard I try, I can't be good.

When we get home, I go straight up to my room. Hilda races after me, following me onto my bed. She sprawls out, resting her head next to mine, panting hot air in my face, like she knows something is wrong and she's trying to protect me.

I unlock my phone and re-read Red's and my texts over and over, looking for clues, because I don't get what happened. Why would he tell Dylan and not me? But I still can't find the answer, and he hasn't written anything new. I need to stop thinking about him, because it's not helping.

I put my phone down and it starts buzzing. It's a text from Sanam: Are you okay?

Not really, I reply. *I messed up.*

It's okay. It was your first tournament. You'll learn to play under pressure.

We lost because of me.

That's not how it works.

That's what everyone probably thinks.

Maybe, she texts. I'm glad she doesn't lie to me. But they're wrong. You weren't the only one who lost. It was a pretty rough day. Red didn't show up in time to play, and Quinn lost all but one game.

I didn't know that, I tell her.

It'll be fine by Monday.

Thanks, I text, because I like that she's trying to make it better. It helps.

I should start my homework, but I'd rather read my new book about the history of magic, so I do that instead. I'll deal with everything hard tomorrow.

NINE.

WHEN MY ALARM goes off on Sunday morning, I pull myself out of bed, shower, and make breakfast. I have a whole plan to get up early and start my homework right away, but as soon as I'm back upstairs, I can't stop thinking about chess. I just want to win a few rounds. I tell myself that I'm only allowed to play for fifteen minutes, and then I'll do my homework at 9:15 a.m. on the dot. Except once I get started, everything around me disappears, and I'm floating and focused and the only thing that matters is solving the challenge in front of me, putting each piece in the right place. I'm on a roll, and I don't want to stop, because it feels good to play like someone who could win again.

The next time I look up at the clock it's 9:36. *Oops.* I guess I'll start my homework at 10:00 instead. Before I realize any time has even passed, it's 9:55. I'm right in the middle of a really hard puzzle that I want to solve, because I'm pretty sure I can, but I know if I don't walk away right now, I'll feel even worse than I do about the fact that it's Sunday at 9:56 and I haven't done any homework. I shut my computer, stand up as fast as I can, and open my closet.

Even though I bought the cutest, happiest backpack I could find, with green and pink flowers, it still looks sad and crumpled, shoved into the corner next to a pair of shoes. I pull out my bag and open my schedule for Monday: math, study hall, Spanish, chess, English, history, and science.

I never know if it's better to do my homework in order from easiest to hardest or vice versa, but today I want to finish math so I don't have word problems hanging over my head. I wander downstairs to look for Dad, because I missed two classes last week and I don't get integers, not even a little, so I really need his help. He's not in the kitchen or the family room, but I can hear him talking, so I follow his voice down the hall toward the small office he shares with Mom. He sounds serious, like something is bad or someone's in trouble. I hope it's not me.

I stop walking right before I get to the office, and lean against the wall.

Mom says, "I'm worried about her."

"I am, too." Dad sighs.

"If she hadn't spent half her weekend at the tournament, she'd have a lot more time for homework."

"How's that fair?" Dad asks.

"It's not," Mom says tersely. "But it's true."

"Maybe."

I swallow hard.

"The reality is chess is taking up a lot of time and energy she could be spending on schoolwork," Mom says. "I know she loves playing and I want her to be able to do everything she loves, but chess can't be the priority right now. It's not like she's going to be a professional chess player. I really think if she had more time to study, help from Ms. Curtis, and medication, school would be less overwhelming."

Dad sighs again. I hold my breath and wait for him to say something else—to defend me. "I agree with you," he says. "I have to jump on this call, but we can talk more after."

"I'm not sure there's anything else to say," Mom says. "We have our plan."

I don't wait to see what happens next. I tiptoe as fast as

I can down the hall, up the stairs, and into my room. I open my math textbook and start reading the chapter on integers from the beginning, hoping the information will sink in this time.

When Mom shouts, "Henley? Clea? Time for dinner!" I've only finished half my homework. The last thing I want to do right now is sit across the table from my parents, but I'm hungry, and I need energy to finish everything that's due tomorrow.

The kitchen is warm, and it smells like tomato sauce and melted cheese. Mom waits until we're all sitting before she takes the eggplant parmesan out of the oven and brings it over to the table.

It doesn't matter that Mom says the food is hot and we should let it cool down; as soon as the piece of eggplant parm is on my plate, I take a big bite and burn the roof of my mouth. *UGH.* I don't get why I didn't just listen and wait a few minutes.

The worst part is after that my mouth hurts whenever I eat anything. Even the salad feels like it's cutting into me. I act like I'm taking my time, because I don't want to hear Mom say that she told me so. I already know she's right and I'm wrong, but only about this. She's wrong about chess.

I wait until my food is practically cold to start eating. It's still really good, but the salty cheese stings every time I take a bite.

As we're finishing dinner, the phone rings. Henley jumps up and runs over to answer it. "Hello," she says into the receiver. Then she looks at me. "It's for you."

I have no idea who would call my house, other than—*oh no*. I really hope it's not Mr. Lee telling me that he's never seen a worse performance in his life, and even though every seventh grader is technically allowed to be on the team, he's suggesting I quit, because I'm that bad.

Henley hands me the phone and then sits back down.

"Hello?" My voice is so quiet I hardly recognize it.

The person on the other end is breathing hard, and it sounds like whoever it is might be hyperventilating. "Can you come over? Please." Red's words spill out of him, between gasps. "You didn't pick up your phone. I'm sorry I didn't tell you." He pauses to breathe. "I'm grounded. I can't leave. But you can come here. My mom said—"

"Red, I'm coming over—right now," I say. "Just stay where you are, okay?"

"Okay," he says.

"Promise?" I ask, because Red has run away before, when

153

he first found out his parents were splitting up. It was bad. His mom had to call the police.

"I'm nodding," he says.

When I look up, Mom is getting her car keys. I don't have to say anything; she knows exactly where I'm going. And even though it's only a few streets away, the sun is going down, and I know she doesn't want me walking to his house at dusk.

Mom and I are both silent on the ride to Red's house. But when she parks the car in his driveway, she grabs on to me and pulls me in as close to her as she can. "I love you, Clea," she says. "And I'm very proud of you. You're a good friend."

All of a sudden, I wonder if maybe—"You know about Red's dad—and the baby?" I ask before I can stop the words from falling out of my mouth.

She nods. And I realize that if Mom knows then eventually other people will know, too, and they'll talk about Red and his family and how everything is a mess. I have no clue what I could ever say to him to make this okay. "Red is going through something really hard," Mom says. "But he knows he can count on you to be there for him."

"I don't even know what to say."

"Then listen and let him talk about whatever he's feeling. That will help."

"What if it doesn't?" I ask.

"It will," Mom says. "Maybe not today. It's going to take time for Red to process everything that's happened with his dad. But being there for him right now, when he's in pain, will help him, because no matter how bad he feels, he knows he's not alone."

"Okay," I say. "I get it."

"Good," she says. "Promise you'll call me if you need anything."

"I promise."

Mom hugs me again, holding on tight, and then kisses my forehead.

I get out of the car and knock on the front door. Red's sister, Edie, answers. Her strawberry-blond hair is in a huge, floppy bun at the top of her head that makes her look cool and casual.

"He's in the basement," she says. And before I can say anything, she's gone.

I take my shoes off and leave my jacket on, zipping it all the way up to my chin. It's cold inside, and the lights are off. It feels emptier and sadder than usual. Red lives in the kind of house where everything is white and beige and no one ever spills. They never have eggplant parm with red sauce for

155

dinner. There's no clutter or pictures or anything that indicates people actually live here. The furniture reminds me of marshmallows and spaceships put together, and all I can think about is what it would feel like to take one of Henley's purple markers and draw hearts all over everything.

When I get down to the basement, Red is slumped on the couch, sinking between white leather cushions. I sit down on the empty half of the sofa and face him, crossing my legs into a pretzel. He looks small and deflated, like everything happy has been drained out of him. I'm afraid that if he sinks any farther into the fluffy cushions, he might fade away completely.

"Dylan told you, right?" His voice cracks.

"Yeah." I nod. I still want to know why he didn't tell me, but I can't ask him now.

"Does everyone know?" he asks.

"I really don't know. I mean, my mom knew why I was coming over, and I didn't say anything. But maybe your mom told my mom."

"I was just starting to get used to how bad everything was," he says. "I hated that he moved to Colorado with Barf, but deep down I knew we were more important. Kids come first. But now—" He shakes his head. "He's going to have a new kid and a new family. And it feels like they're more important than us, or at least the same amount of important. We already have to share everything else with her. I just wanted one thing that was ours."

Red can't hold his tears back. I reach out and take his hand. It's a little too warm, like he's overheating. I want to scream for him, because it's not fair and I hate that this is happening, but I don't, because I know that won't help.

We sit in the almost dark for a while, until Red stops crying and closes his eyes. When he opens them again, he says, "I really wish I didn't care what he did. Then it wouldn't hurt so much."

"He's your dad—I'm pretty sure it's impossible not to care."

"Edie doesn't."

"She acts like she doesn't," I say. "But you know she cares."

"She's really good at pretending our dad doesn't bother her," he says. "I wish I could do that. I bet it would make everything way easier."

"Yeah, but I think it's probably better to be honest about what's actually happening, even if it is harder."

"Maybe," he says. "The worst part is that it doesn't even matter that I hate him. He gets to start all over with a brandnew baby. He doesn't need me."

"I don't think that's how it works," I say.

He shrugs.

"I'm sorry," I say. "It's not fair."

"Thanks for coming over."

"Always. No matter what."

"I know. But—thanks."

Everything is still bad, but I can tell it's going to get better.

TEN.

IN THE MORNING, Mom, Dad, and I go to Dr. Gold's office.

Dad leaves his luggage in the car, but I know it's there. I can't stop thinking about the fact that he's leaving in a few hours and won't be home again until Friday. That's so many days from now. And even though he's sitting next to me in the quiet waiting room, I miss him already.

I don't want to be here. There's no point, since Mom and Dad already decided, and the cold, hard truth is that they don't really care what I think. They just want my problem to go away and I do, too, but it's not happening. I hate that right now I'm missing math, since I actually finished all of my homework.

After Mom picked me up from Red's house last night, I did English, math, and Spanish, but I fell asleep before I could start history or science. I tried to wake up early this morning, but I didn't have enough time to get through the directions before we had to leave. My grand plan is to go to the library during lunch and do both assignments in forty-five minutes. And even though I sort of know that's impossible, I have to find a way to make it happen.

My phone buzzes in my bag. It's a text from Red. Where are you?

Late. Be there post-math, I write back, because even though I'm happy he noticed that I'm not at school, I don't feel like talking about where I am or what's going on right now. I feel like throwing up in my mouth.

Okay, he says. Cool.

At 7:30 on the dot, the door to Dr. Gold's office swings open, like she was standing on the other side, waiting for the clock to change. "Good morning." She smiles at me and then at Mom and Dad. "Come on in." Dr. Gold is wearing a navy-blue dress with white polka dots and a belt with a big red flower that matches her mood. I'm wearing all black, which tells the story of how *I* feel.

It's silent as we all shuffle into her office and sit down.

"Before we get started, I wanted to reassure you that Dr. Sharma reviewed your test again and the results are still the same," Dr. Gold says to me.

"Thank you," I respond, because even though it's really hard for me to believe that I'm not stupid, the fact that Dr. Gold had my score double-checked makes me trust her even more. "I don't even know why I'm here," I continue. I can feel Mom and Dad staring at me, waiting for me to explain myself. But I don't take my eyes off Dr. Gold, because she's the only person in this room who I'm not mad at right now. "There's no point to me being at this meeting. It's basically a huge waste of time. And I don't want to miss any more school. They're just going to do what they want to do," I say, pointing to my parents.

"*Clea*—" Mom says my name like she wants me to stop talking right now.

"No, Mom," I say back. "I heard every single thing you said about me, so don't even try to deny it. No offense, but it wasn't that smart to have a private conversation about me in the middle of the house. Next time—maybe try whispering."

Mom doesn't say anything. She sits there, looking hurt, like I did something awful to her, when it's really the other way around.

"Okay, let's take a step back," Dr. Gold says. "Clea, I'd like you to explain what you heard and how it made you feel. And Mom and Dad, I'd like you to listen without responding until Clea is finished, even if what she shares is different from what you said or intended to say. You'll have a chance to respond after. Does that work?"

"Yes," I say. I don't look over at Mom and Dad, but I can see them nodding out of the corner of my eye. "Okay, so basically it was like (A) If I had enough time for my homework, I'd be doing fine in school. But I don't, because of chess. All my problems are because of chess. Blame chess. (B) There's no chance I'm ever going pro, because I'm bad at chess—"

"I never said you were bad at chess," Mom says.

I roll my eyes, because she didn't have to say it. It was *implied*.

"Let's give Clea a chance to finish," Dr. Gold jumps in to stop Mom, and then she looks back at me, like she wants me to know it's still my turn. It feels good to have her take my side over Mom's, because she's an adult and a doctor and super important. It makes me feel like I'm important, too.

"(C) If I do exactly what they want and I stop chess, everything will be totally fixed." I take a deep breath. "As for how it made me feel—well, right now I feel like I'm so stupid and like there's something really wrong with me, because I had all day yesterday to finish my homework, and I didn't have that much or anything big and I really tried. And I'm pretty sure I suck at chess. I mean, after all this time, I finally got picked to play in a tournament, and then I messed up by being an idiot and thinking about Red and all the noises instead of focusing and winning my games. So you're right about everything. I hope you're happy."

"That definitely doesn't make me happy," Mom says.

"Yeah, right. Just admit you hate chess and you can't wait to take it away from me."

She sighs. "I can't understand how sometimes you can be so capable and focused, and other times you're exactly the opposite. I'm sorry, but it's very hard for me to believe that you're not deciding when you feel like concentrating and when you don't. And if that can be fixed, I would be thrilled."

"You're not sorry," I say. "Don't lie. You think I'm not

trying hard enough and that I'm the problem. And guess what? Surprise! *I think that, too.*"

Mom doesn't say anything.

Dr. Gold looks right at me and nods a lot, like she wants me to know that she's heard everything and she's sorry. "The fact that ADHD manifests in extremes can make it very frustrating and difficult for everyone, even the person with ADHD, to understand and accept reality." Dr. Gold looks at Mom and then at me. "ADHD doesn't mean you can't focus. It means you have a hard time shifting, maintaining, and controlling attention and emotion, because the part of your brain that handles self-regulation is wired differently. Sometimes your gears get stuck and you can't stop thinking about one thing and other times the gears are out of control, switching so quickly you can't pause and do just one thing."

"Is that why I couldn't stop worrying about Red when I was supposed to be playing chess? Or hearing the person next to me chewing gum?" I ask.

She nods. "Can you remember an experience when the gears were constantly shifting?"

"Um, yeah," I say. "That's basically my entire life in a nutshell. I mean, my life when the gears aren't stuck."

Dr. Gold grins, and then she glances over at Mom and

Dad. "I want to make sure you understand what Clea is experiencing."

"I understand in theory," Dad says.

"Me too," Mom says.

"That's a good place to start. Because we can't see Clea's ADHD, it's easy to think that it's not a big deal. It's not really happening. Or what I've heard from all of you a lot—Clea needs to try harder, because she's capable. The problem with that thought pattern is when she isn't able to switch gears or stop the gears from switching on her, she starts to feel like there's something wrong with her, when in reality, Clea is a very intelligent, thoughtful, hardworking student, daughter, friend, and sister who happens to have ADHD." Dr. Gold looks at me. "It's part of who you are. There are challenges, but there are a lot of benefits."

"Uh, I don't see anything good," I say back.

"You will," Dr. Gold says.

I want to believe her, because I think she's smart and usually right, but I don't.

"It's hard not to get frustrated," Mom says. "All we want is for Clea to be that capable, driven person we know is in there all the time."

"I think it's important in those moments where *you* are

feeling frustrated, to stop and think about how hard it must be for Clea. Even though you can't see Clea's ADHD, try to remember that it's there, recognize the symptoms when they show up, and have compassion for her," Dr. Gold says. "I know it's hard to understand, because sometimes Clea is able to do everyday things easily and other times it feels like she's not able to do the exact same thing."

Mom nods, like she wants Dr. Gold to know that's true.

"But it would be very helpful to Clea if she felt like you trusted that she's trying her best and if you assumed that she's already being hard on herself. She doesn't need help feeling bad, but she does need praise when she tries something that's challenging for her and when she does well."

"That would really help," I say, because I know Dr. Gold is right. "Like today, basically the last thing on earth I want to do is go to chess practice, because I messed everything up for the whole team. I lost three games in a row. And instead of being all negative about chess, like always, it would be better if you could be proud of me for not quitting and going back even though I'm embarrassed."

"We are so proud of you," Mom says. "Really. We are."

Dad nods. "That takes guts."

"It's not like I have a choice. Chess is the only thing

I can be good at, even if you don't think I can be." I look at Mom. "I'm not going to throw all my hard work away because I had one bad tournament. That doesn't seem very smart."

"A lot of people would," Mom says. "It's much easier to quit when things get hard than to try again."

"Maybe," I say, because I think she could be right about that.

"Remember how you said that you couldn't think of anything good about having ADHD?" Dr. Gold asks me. "Persistence is one of those great qualities. You've had to be determined, because you've faced challenges you didn't even realize were in front of you. You've fallen down and had to pick yourself back up a lot. And even though that maybe doesn't seem like a good thing, the more often you fall down, the easier it gets to take the next risk. You know that falling hurts, but also that it's not the end of the world, because you have experience. That's a big advantage."

"But isn't it better just to never fall down at all?" I ask.

"The problem with never failing is that your brain changes and grows in response to challenge, so if everything is easy and you never face anything difficult, you don't have the chance to get stronger or better."

"And that's not good, because then you stay the same?" I ask.

Dr. Gold nods. "Exactly."

"Can you explain how Clea can be good at chess and bad at math?" Mom asks.

"I'm not convinced she's 'bad' at math." Dr. Gold uses her fingers as quotation marks when she says the word *bad*. "And I'd encourage you to try to eliminate words like 'bad' and 'stupid'—fixed descriptors—from the conversation, because they don't reflect reality. Clea's brain, and frankly all of our brains, are still developing and changing, so they aren't one way. When it comes to math, I think following instructions is difficult for Clea, and there are a lot of directions in math homework and tests."

"Oh," Mom says. It seems like she's trying to let the information sink in.

Dr. Gold looks at me. "One reason you're such a great chess player is that your mind is used to overcoming obstacles and thinking differently and creatively to help you succeed, which is why parts of the game are so natural for you. You've had a lifetime of practice."

"Wait—I'm good at chess *because* I have ADHD?" I say.

Dr. Gold nods.

"That's so cool," I tell her.

"I think so, too." She smiles back. "Now, one of the things we talked about last time was medication. Are you still interested in exploring that option?" Dr. Gold asks, looking first at Mom and Dad. They both nod. Then she looks at me. "How do you feel, Clea?"

"I don't want to take medicine."

"Why not?"

"It makes me feel like something is really wrong with me," I say. "And like I have this big problem, and I'm too weak to handle it on my own."

"That's what you've been doing—handling everything by yourself, and considering that you've had no help or information, you've been doing an excellent job. I think you need to give yourself credit for that. I understand why it might feel like you're weak if you admit that you need help with your ADHD, and also I understand that taking a pill to help you might make it feel bigger than you want it to be. But I think it's exactly the opposite. It's very hard for all of us to face up to our challenges—and, trust me, we all have them—but choosing to do that makes you strong and it will make your ADHD smaller and less important, because even though it will still be there, you won't be constantly coming up against it."

169

"If I try taking medicine and I don't like how it feels, do I have to keep taking it?" I ask.

"You can stop immediately," she says. "If that happens, your parents will give me a call right away, and we'll meet and talk about what happened. And if you try the medicine, and you're experiencing positive changes, I'd still want to meet with you after two weeks to check in and see how everything is going."

"Then I'd feel okay about trying medicine to see if it works," I say. "I mean, right now, I'd probably try anything, because I think I really need help."

When I get to school, math is basically over, so I go to the bathroom for a few minutes and reapply my tinted lip gloss while I wait for the bell to ring. I have study hall next, aka my first meeting with Ms. Curtis. And even though I'm excited to finally have a plan, I'm afraid she won't be able help me and I'm so far behind that there's nothing anyone can do to make school okay.

The bell rings, and I walk down the hallway toward Ms. Curtis's office. Classroom doors swing open and seventh graders start flooding into the hall. I don't want to see anyone from the team, because I'm pretty sure after what happened at the tournament everyone is talking about how bad I am at chess, and I don't need to feel any worse than I already do about how I played.

"Clea." I recognize Red's voice before I look up and see him standing by the lockers, smiling at me. "Where's your shirt?"

That's when I realize he's wearing his chess team jersey, which means I'm supposed to be wearing mine, too—because today is the raffle. "I forgot."

"Everyone's going to think you quit the team," he says.

"But I didn't."

"That doesn't matter." He drops his backpack, pulls his chess team jersey over his head, and adjusts the navy-blue T-shirt he has on underneath. "Wear mine. I'll say I forgot." He hands me his shirt like he doesn't care that I flopped in the tournament and humiliated myself in front of everyone. He still wants to be on a team with me. "I'll see you at lunch. We signed up for twelve fifteen."

"I remember that part."

"Cool," he says and walks away, down the hall toward his next class.

I put my bag on the floor, pull Red's shirt over my head, and slip my arms through the sleeves, just in case I walk by anyone from the team between now and lunch.

When I get to Ms. Curtis's office, she's standing by the door, scanning her big bookshelf, and holding a stack of papers.

"Clea, welcome." Ms. Curtis has the kind of soothing voice that makes me think she's probably good at singing Disney songs. "Make yourself comfortable." She points to the round table and chairs in the back of the room and puts down the papers in her hand.

I'm not sure why, but it doesn't feel like I'm in school anymore. I've been transported someplace else where the walls aren't white and regular. They're pale blue, like the sky on a warm summer morning, and the floor is almost entirely covered up by a rug the color of wheat. There are cloth bins stacked in perfect rows. Everything is so organized that the room feels empty and clean and brand-new. Ms. Curtis doesn't have sticky notes or a mug that says *World's Best Teacher* stuffed with mismatched pencils on her desk. There are two identical notebooks and one blue pen, which she brings with her when she sits down next to me.

Something about Ms. Curtis reminds me of Samantha from *Bewitched*. I guess maybe I hope she's a little like her, too, and that she has magic powers to make things better for me, because that's all I want. I'm tired of everything being hard.

172

"I'm so glad you're here." She tucks her caramel-colored hair behind her ears and then ties it back into a low ponytail. "I just spoke with your mom, and will be talking to Dr. Gold again later today, to make sure we're all on the same page. I think having an education plan is going to help you a lot."

I want to tell Ms. Curtis that I love her office and I wish every room I ever walked into made me feel this way—calm and under control, and like I'm going to be okay. Except nothing has happened yet, and I'm too afraid to jinx it, so I smile and say, "I hope so."

"Part of this process is giving you new tools and strategies to make school more manageable." She places a notebook in front of me. "This is your new weekly planner. I've included your schedule for the rest of the semester, and there are color-coded spaces next to each class where you can write down your assignments—yellow for homework, blue for papers, and green for tests. We'll transfer everything from your old planner while you're here today to make sure nothing gets lost in the transition." There are typed-up reminders on each page. I'm afraid to even touch the notebook, because I'm sure as soon as I do I'll mess it up. "Also, you are allowed to have extended time for quizzes, tests, and in-class assignments.

I've let your teachers know about the new accommodation. But you'll need to be the one to ask for the extra time."

"Okay," I say. "Are you going to be able to fix me?"

"I know school has been hard for you lately," she says.

"I want to stop messing up."

"Can you give me an example of one thing you feel you've messed up?" It surprises me that she doesn't tell me it's okay or I'm not as bad as I think. It feels like she's taking me seriously.

"I forgot that the chess team raffle was today at lunch, and I didn't wear my shirt. This is Red's," I say. "And that's when I was planning to do my history and science homework, because I didn't have enough time this weekend to finish."

"It sounds like dominoes," she says. "One piece falls, and everything else comes crashing down."

I nod.

"The reason you forget about things is that ADHD impacts your working memory. In your planner, there is a blank section. I want you to keep a list every week of anything you hear someone say that you need to remember to do. Get used to scribbling it down so you have a visual reminder."

"Like in chess, how we have to keep a record of every move we make."

174

"Exactly. All that practice will help you," she says. "I'm going to ask you to implement four strategies tonight when you get home from school." She points to a typed page that she's stapled into my planner. "First, I'd like you to start your homework with a subject you love or an assignment where you feel like you can succeed."

"Why is that better?" I ask.

"If you start with something challenging and you don't make a lot of progress, you're not going to want to do the rest of your homework."

"Oh yeah," I say. "Duh."

"I want you to work in thirty-minute increments and set alarms for yourself, so you remember to stop. This will keep you from getting distracted for too long and help you switch gears when you need to move to the next thing."

"I can do that," I say, because I know exactly what she means.

"While you're working, if you have a phone, I want you to put it on *do not disturb* to eliminate unnecessary distractions. And finally, I'd like you to use this." She stands up and walks over to her desk. Then she opens one of the drawers, takes out a small balloon, and gives it to me. It's filled with sand. I move it around in my hand. "Fidgeting actually stimulates your brain, so playing with the balloon will help you stay focused. You can use it while you're doing homework and during class to help you concentrate. What do you think?"

"I'm not trying to be rude, but it doesn't seem like any of these things are going to help that much."

"They will," she promises.

When the bell rings for lunch, all I want to do is hide out in the library, where it's safe and I don't have to think about how badly I messed up in the tournament. I'd rather avoid the cafeteria and the chess team until everyone has a chance to forget that I'm the reason we lost . . . but I can't let anyone think I quit.

There's a big crowd around the entrance to the cafeteria, where a folding table is set up for the raffle. The prizes are all on display, and there's a white foam board with green letters and gold sparkles that says:

2, 4, 6, 8, FIRST IT'S CHECK, AND THEN IT'S MATE.
ENTER THE CHESS TEAM RAFFLE NOW. YOU MIGHT WIN BIG!
BEST PRIZES EVER, EVER, EVER!!!

I know Quinn made the poster as soon as I see it. She's smiling and pointing to the different prizes, acting like she's the queen bee of chess. All we had last year were free ice-skating passes and a gigantic bucket of jelly beans. But this year Quinn's dad donated these special Patriots tickets in a box with other fancy football things, and now everyone in the entire middle school is lining up for a chance to win. She twirls the end of her long blond locks, soaking in the attention. She has this look on her face like she's happy and also like she just ate a handful of yellow Sour Patch Kids.

I walk by the crowd of people waiting to buy tickets. I have fifteen minutes to eat before Red and I take over for Quinn. When I get to our table in the back corner of the cafeteria, Red is there with Dylan, which is new and not normal. Dylan usually sits with Isaac in the middle of everything.

"We were just talking about chess camp," Red says as soon as I sit down. "I can't believe it's in three weeks."

I can't, either, but I don't say that, because I don't need to remind him that I forget about everything. I'm already wearing his jersey.

"Mr. Lee said Katerina is teaching a chess clinic for the top twelve." Dylan pushes his floppy hair out of his eyes.

"Shut up," Red says. "What about everyone else?"

"I didn't listen to that part. Sorry." Dylan looks at me.

"We still have three weeks of practice and two tournaments

before camp. A lot can happen," Red says. "You can turn things around."

"Dude," Dylan says. "Don't lie to her."

"I'm not."

"You are. But whatever."

"So, if that's a lie, what's the truth?" I ask, because I want to know, even if it hurts. And I can count on Dylan not to care about my feelings.

"Mr. Lee isn't going to play you in a tourney, because he just did, and—" He stops himself. "He wants to win. So practice is your only chance to show him that he was right to pick you in the first place. You have to do something major."

"Like what?" I ask.

"Take a risk. I'd mix in some coffeehouse moves."

"No way," Red says. "He'll think you're unreliable."

"Not if you win." Dylan looks at me. "It's just a riskier style of chess that uses tricks. I'm not saying cheat or act stupid, but if you really want to train with Katerina—"

"I do!" I say.

"Then you need to show him you're not afraid to be creative and that what happened at the tournament wasn't who you are as a player. Worst case—it doesn't work. At least you tried something. Whatever you do, don't play it safe, or you'll have zero chance of getting picked."

"I don't even know where to start learning coffeehouse moves," I say.

"I have a book. My brother bought it for me," Dylan says. "You can, um, borrow it, if you want."

"Yes," I say. "Thanks."

"No problem." He smiles at me, and my stomach drops, which is weird. And right now it seems like everything is flipped, because Red is wrong and Dylan is the one who's helping me and saying exactly what I need to hear.

I drink the rest of my milk and force down a banana and half of my sandwich, because I need energy for chess. I have to win today.

After we finish eating, we walk over to the raffle table. I can't see what's happening, because there's a crowd of people waiting to buy tickets, but I can hear Quinn say, "Step right up. Support the chess team. We're really good this year!"

"If by really good, you mean you lost your big tournament." It's Vivi.

"It wasn't our fault," Quinn says.

"Didn't you lose, like, every round?" Vivi asks.

"Um, no. That was Clea. She bombed. I don't know why

179

she got picked. She's not even good," Quinn says. "I think it was, like, charity or something."

My heart stops.

"She must be so embarrassed," Vivi says.

"Who cares? We're the ones who have to pick up her slack and win the rest of our tournaments if we want a shot at the championship, which we obviously do," Quinn says. "She should really quit. She's already done enough damage."

I feel my heart in my throat.

"It's not Clea's fault we lost. And she's not quitting," Red says. "It was her first tournament."

Everyone turns to look at us.

"And her last." Quinn smirks.

"You wish," he says. "You're just mad because she's good and she keeps getting better, unlike some other people on the team."

"Please. Whatever." Quinn rolls her eyes. "At least I showed up on time. I mean, seriously. What were you even doing?"

Red doesn't say anything. I can't just stand here and let her talk to him like that.

"He was a few minutes late. So what? Get over it." My mind is racing, spinning so fast that the words are out of my

180

mouth before I can find the brakes to slow down and stop them from coming out the way they do—fast and harsh. "You seriously have no clue."

"No, Clea, that's you. It's like you can't help yourself. You just keep messing up." Quinn laughs. "Maybe you should stop hanging out with Red. I think you're contagious."

"And I think if your dad got married and didn't invite you to the wedding and then showed up right before the tournament to tell you he's having another baby, you would have been late, too." I don't realize what I'm saying until the words are already out of my mouth and it's too late. All I want to do is suck everything I just said back in like spaghetti.

Someone gasps, and a few people giggle and whisper, murmuring loudly to each other. I look at Red, but his eyes are glued to the floor.

"Awkward," Quinn says, dragging the word through the air. "I hate to break up this little pity party, but it's twelve fifteen, so it's your turn to be in charge of the raffle," she says. "Bye!"

I walk over to the folding table, like I'm ready to take over. Red doesn't follow behind me. He keeps his head down and walks out of the cafeteria with Dylan. There's a lump in the back of my throat getting bigger, making it hard for me to breathe. I want to run after him and tell him how sorry I am and promise I'll never do anything like that ever again. But Quinn is gone, and there's no one left to sell tickets. And I can't ruin things for the team—again.

When I look up, Sanam is standing next to me. I hope she didn't hear what I said. I don't want her to think I'm the kind of friend who can't keep a secret, because I haven't told anyone about her crush on Red. But by the way she's looking at me, with strained, sad eyes, I'm sure she heard everything. "Need help?" she asks.

I nod. I want to say thank you, but I'm afraid if I say anything, everything I'm feeling will come pouring out of me, and I can't let that happen.

After our fifteen minutes are up, we hand the table over to Lily and Layla, and walk outside. Dylan is in the courtyard with a big crew, but Red isn't there, or on our bench, or on the field playing soccer. He isn't anywhere, and I have this horrible sinking feeling in my stomach that he's avoiding me.

We still have ten minutes before electives, so Sanam and I sit on the grass by the playground. The leaves on the trees around the perimeter of school are orange and yellow and red and starting to fall in scattered clumps, and the air is cold, even in the sun. "We didn't lose because of you," Sanam says.

"No one thinks that, except for Quinn, and she's wrong. She makes fun of people who are in her way, like you and me, because we're really good at chess."

"*You* are," I say.

"Trust me, if she thought you had no chance of beating her, she'd ignore you like she did last year."

"I don't know," I say and tug at the grass.

"I do." She says it like it's a fact that won't change. "What happened back there with Red? Why did you say all that stuff?"

"I didn't mean to. I was trying to stand up for him."

"Well, I know," she says. "That was obvious. But you kind of went too far. Is everything okay?"

I'm going to tell her now. I want to. "It's like—I lost control," I say. "I think it has to do with my, um, ADHD."

"I didn't know you had that," she says.

"Me neither. I found out last week."

"Wow. Seriously? I thought I was the only one on the team—"

"Wait—you have ADHD, too?"

"Well, no, I have dyslexia and—"

"What? But you're so good at school."

"I work really hard," she says. "And I usually meet with a

183

tutor at lunch. We practice reading and she helps me with homework, so that makes a lot of things easier. Not reading out loud or writing on the board. But mostly everything else is okay."

"Oh," I say. "I thought you were in a special language class."

"I am." She smiles and fiddles with the zipper on her jacket. "I wasn't trying to hide it from you. I guess I don't really talk about being dyslexic that much, because it's part of me. I mean, I've known about it since first grade. And tutoring is what I need to do so that it doesn't get in my way."

"That's what my doctor said about meeting with Ms. Curtis and taking medicine. If I do those things, having ADHD will get easier for me."

"It definitely will," she says. "I seriously can't believe you just found out. It would be like if this whole time I thought I was totally regular, but the letters were all mixed up in my head and moving around whenever I was reading or writing, and no one else knew about it except for me. Only I thought it was like that for everyone else, too, but I was just slower and not as good."

"Yes! That's exactly what it's like," I tell her. "Except I

thought I was dumb and lazy and not trying hard enough and that's why I couldn't finish my work or follow directions or stop my brain from getting distracted."

"That must be so hard," she says. "It's like out of nowhere everything you thought about yourself before right now is totally wrong, because you didn't have all the information. If I were you, I wouldn't be able to think about anything else."

"I've been trying not to think about ADHD, because it feels like an excuse for why I'm bad at everything. But it's like no matter what I do, it's always getting in my way. And not just in school."

"You're making it seem like your ADHD is fake or like you could shut it off if you wanted to, when you can't. And the fact that you didn't know about it is the reason everything's been so hard."

I like the way Sanam talks about ADHD. She makes it seem important and like it's okay for me to be mad that no one noticed I needed help for way too long, which feels good, because I am. "I can't believe I did that to Red—in front of everyone."

"Does he know you have it?" she asks.

"Yeah."

"Good. I feel like that might help when you apologize."

"I really hope you're right."

"Me too," she says.

I have to ask: "You seriously don't think it's my fault that we lost the tournament?"

"No way," she says. "Mr. Lee wouldn't have picked you if you weren't a really strong player. He just doesn't do that."

I nod and try to let her words sink in.

She continues. "So what if you got distracted because it was your first tournament and you kind of have a lot going on right now? Don't blame yourself for the whole tournament and get psyched out when you've gotten this far. That'd be such a waste."

"True," I say, because I'm pretty sure Sanam is right—everything I thought about myself before now is wrong, and I guess I still need to get used to seeing myself in this new way. But I really want to.

Red shows up three minutes late to practice and sits on the other side of the room next to Dylan, even though there's an empty seat by me.

"Today I want to talk about open files, half-open files, and batteries by looking at how you can set up your rooks to work together in order to control the board," Mr. Lee says.

I open my notebook and start writing everything down, but I keep glancing over at Red, waiting for him to look back at me. He stays still and statuesque, arms crossed, like he can just listen and remember.

Mr. Lee hangs up the demonstration chessboard, which is good. It helps me to have a visual while he talks through strategy.

Once he's done teaching, we only have twenty-five minutes left. "Let's play with ten minutes on the clock," he says. "Quickly pair up and get to it."

As soon as Mr. Lee finishes, Quinn stands up and bolts across the room and over to Sanam, like she's on a mission.

Normally I love when Mr. Lee lets us pick, because it's basically the only time Red and I ever get to play against each other. I automatically look over at him, because we're partners in everything—it's a reflex. But he's sitting across from Dylan. He doesn't even glance in my direction. I know I just need to apologize, because I really am sorry, and then everything will be better. It always is. It has to be.

Everyone else is already paired up. I don't move, because I don't know where to go. There's no one left.

Mr. Lee walks over to me with a chessboard. "We're an odd number today," he says and sits down across from me.

The only person who's volunteering to be my partner is the teacher. *Great. Just great.*

I can see his *The Lord of the Rings* T-shirt under his button-down teacher shirt.

Mr. Lee starts the game.

I make my move, tap the clock, and write down what I just did.

We go back and forth, and I feel pretty good about how I'm playing because I get him into check once, but Mr. Lee wins.

When the bell rings, everyone starts to clear out of the room.

"Clea," Mr. Lee says, stopping me before I can stand up and walk away. "I wanted to check in with you about the tournament."

"I'm sorry," I say. "You gave me a chance and I—" Even if I wasn't the only reason we lost, I was one of the reasons we didn't win. "I'm going to play a lot better next time—if you ever pick me again. I love chess."

"I know you do," he says. "I'm glad to hear that you aren't discouraged after Saturday. It can be hard to lose, but it always helps me to remember that even the best players have days like that. I'm happy to tell you all about the times I lost big when I was playing competitively."

"I thought you were a National Master," I say, because now I'm confused. Maybe I had the wrong information about Mr. Lee's ranking.

"I was. But I still lost a lot. That's how I learned to be good," he says. "The players who gave up or were afraid to fail ended up being average. If you want to be great, you have to learn from every game and push yourself to improve. That's the reason we write everything down, so we can review where we got tripped up and use those mistakes to our advantage later. We have to take risks and get things wrong to develop and become smart players. Good chess players are persistent."

"I'm persistent," I say, remembering what Dr. Gold said about me.

"You are," he says. "And you have great instincts."

"Thanks." I grin, because it feels good that Mr. Lee believes in me and thinks failing makes you better and smarter. It's awesome news for me, because I do it a lot.

At dismissal, Red is standing by himself. I look around to make sure Dylan is gone and take a deep breath before I walk up to him. "Can I, um, talk to you?" I ask.

"I'd rather you didn't," he says. "But it doesn't seem like you care what I want—so talk, don't talk, do whatever."

189

"I'm really, really sorry."

"I need my jersey," he says.

I drop my backpack, and even though it's cold out, I take off my coat and then his shirt. Before I have a chance to thank him for letting me wear it, he grabs it from me and walks away.

Mom asks a lot of questions on the ride home. She wants to know how everything went with Ms. Curtis and how I'm feeling after our meeting with Dr. Gold. I tell her about my new planner and the four things Ms. Curtis asked me to do tonight. And how I'm excited that school is going to get better. I like knowing I have a plan and a person I can talk to. I think that's going to help.

When we get home, I go straight to my room. All I want to do is call Red and say I'm sorry again, because I am and I want to make sure he heard me. But I know I should wait until I finish my homework, because if I call him now and he doesn't pick up, I'll spend the rest of the night staring at my phone willing him to call me back, which never works.

I take out my planner and open the checklist I made today with Ms. Curtis. I start with Spanish, because I love writing en español and imagining I'm someone else who is happy living in España, eating tapas super-duper late at night, instead of boring American food at 6:30 p.m.

I set my alarm and hold on to the balloon filled with sand, squeezing the squishy ball between my fingers as I read the directions out loud twice, like Ms. Curtis said I should. It's weird how doing something with my hands makes it so much easier for me to focus and for the words to sink into my brain. When my alarm starts blaring thirty minutes later, I'm done with everything on the worksheet, even the extra credit question. I check Spanish off my list, set my next alarm, and start working on history and then math. Check! Check!

Dad calls during dinner to see how the rest of my day went. I tell him about my meeting with Ms. Curtis and about what Mr. Lee said to me during chess. "That's incredible, Clea. I'm so proud of you." Dad sounds happy. "All your hard work is going to pay off. I know it." It feels good to have Dad and Mom on my side.

After dinner, I go back up to my room, but it's hard for me to start working again, especially because I don't feel like studying for my vocabulary test, which is exactly why I saved it for last. But I don't want to call Red until I'm finished with everything, so I set my alarm and force myself to practice for thirty minutes and then for another thirty minutes and another.

I take a break after each alarm. Then I practice every word two more times to make sure I really have them memorized.

When I'm officially done studying, I call Red. The phone only rings three times before it goes to voice mail, like he saw my name and pressed *ignore* on purpose. I leave a message:

"Hi, it's me, Clea. I'm sorry I said all that stuff about your family today in front of everyone. That was so stupid. I promise I won't do anything like that ever again. You don't have to call me back if you don't want to. I just wanted you to know."

I keep my phone next to me for the rest of the night, in case Red calls back. He doesn't.

ELEVEN.

WHEN MY ALARM goes off in the morning, I check my phone. There are no missed calls or texts from Red. I know I said he didn't have to call me back, but I sort of thought he would anyway, because we've never had a fight that went into the next day. It's weird that I'm going to start taking medicine for ADHD, and Red doesn't even know.

The kitchen is warmer than the rest of the house. Mom has made a feast of my favorite foods—blueberry pancakes, smoothies, scrambled eggs, and crispy hash browns.

"Can we please have this every day?" Henley points to her plate. "It's fancy like at a hotel. Pretty please?"

"Maybe." Mom smiles and kisses the top of her head.

Then she sits down next to me and rubs my back with her hand as I finish the last of my strawberry-and-banana smoothie. "The medicine is going to start working quickly, and it will last all day. Remember you might not be very hungry, at least for the first few weeks, but it's important for you to try to eat as much as you can. Your brain needs nutrients to learn."

I haven't even taken the pill yet, and I'm already nervous and not that hungry. "I'm scared," I say softly.

"I know, honey, but try not to worry. It's going to help," Mom says. She holds out a glass of orange juice and a small blue capsule. I put the pill on my tongue, take a sip of juice, and swallow. It tastes sweet and hopeful and like everything is going to get better.

By the time I get to school, my mouth is dry, like I've been eating peanut butter and cotton. It doesn't matter how much water I drink. There isn't enough to unclog my throat, and I'm queasy and carsick from the short ride.

Red isn't waiting for me at our bench, and I guess it's not our bench anymore, because he's never there. He's on the other side of the courtyard, and even though I'm pretty sure he's waiting for Dylan and not me, I walk over to him.

Only, as soon as I'm standing next to him, I have no clue

what to say. And out of nowhere, he feels far away. Like there's this giant balloon between us, and I'm realizing for the first time that it's been there for a while, getting bigger and pushing us farther apart, and now that I know it's there, all I want to do is pop it so everything can go back to normal and we can be best friends again the way we were before this year. "I'm sorry," I say again.

"You should be." He looks at the parking lot and the building and the people in front of us, everywhere but at me.

"I didn't mean to say all those things out loud or make it harder for you."

"I get that you feel bad and you didn't mean to freak out, but it doesn't matter, because that's exactly what you did, and you do it all the time." I'm about to interrupt, because I don't do it *that often*, but I bite down on my lip instead. "You blurt things out. And I get that you were trying to defend me, but I didn't want people to know about the baby, and you knew that. I don't want to keep reminding everyone that my family is a mess. I need school to be normal, because the rest of my life is really bad."

"I know. I'm sorry," I say. "I won't do that ever again. I promise."

"Don't. It's just the way you are. You've always been like

that, and it never mattered before, because nothing in my life was that big of a deal, so if you told people something I didn't want them to know, I didn't care that much. But it's different now—I'm different. And you're the same."

My heart is pounding so hard against my chest. I want to scream, because everything Red just said is true. I take a deep breath. "I'm going to be different starting today. Really."

"How?" he asks, like he definitely doesn't believe me.

"I started taking medicine for ADHD, so I'm going to be in control from now on. I swear—" I try to think of something important to swear on, because I need him to trust me. Best friends trust each other. "On Henley."

"Oh." He sounds surprised, and maybe a little sad that there's something about me that he doesn't know, because I didn't tell him. "When did you start taking medicine?"

"Today," I say. "My parents and the doctor think it's definitely going to help."

"Okay, but I don't get what blurting stuff out has to do with ADHD," he says.

"I guess the same part of your brain that controls attention is in charge of emotions, too, and I need extra help not saying everything I'm thinking."

"I didn't know that," he says. "What's it like so far?"

196

"I'm really thirsty." I take a sip from my water bottle. "But I think it might be working, because when you said all that stuff about how I blurt things out, I didn't interrupt you or anything, and I'm pretty sure that's not how I usually act."

"Wow," he says. "I didn't think of that, but you're right."

"Yeah. It's definitely working," I say, because I need that to be true, and not just because of school and chess, but because everything Red said about me before is right and real, and I wish it weren't. I don't want to be the kind of friend who makes things harder when they're already bad. I want to be someone he can trust.

"Just don't do it anymore, okay?"

"Okay," I say. I'm not going to act like that ever again.

When I get to English, I slide into the empty desk in the front row next to Sanam. My stomach is cramping, and my head is pounding. I pick up my water bottle and drink as much as I can.

"Take one and pass it on," Mr. Lee says and hands me a stack of tests.

I put one on my desk, turn around, and give the pile to Quinn. I write my name at the top of the page. The test is thick. The flimsy staple can barely hold the pages together.

197

"You have thirty minutes to finish," Mr. Lee says. "Good luck."

I do my best to concentrate on the problem in front of me, instead of worrying about all the questions I have to answer before time is up. It feels a little like a switch has been flipped, like all the teeny tiny sounds and smells and movements that would normally pull my attention away have disappeared. But my stomach hurts, like it's empty. Only it's not. I ignore the pain. I read the next word—*sanguine*—and start writing down the definition. *Noun: A bloodred color. Adjective: A* . . . I know this. I do. I'm ready. I practiced this one a lot. I try as hard as I can to remember, except between my head and stomach, I feel like I might puke up the big breakfast I ate all over my desk.

The answer will come to me. I just need to move on to the next one for now: *Vapid. Adjective: Bland. Offering nothing stimulating.* I scribble the definition from memory. *Example sentence: Some people love baseball, but I think sports are vapid.* The words are making me queasy. I lift my head up, hoping to feel better, but it's worse. I'm dizzy and nauseous. I look back down at my test. The medicine is helping me focus. It's working right now. I need to stop making excuses.

By the time Mr. Lee says, "Five more minutes," I'm still on the first page.

I flip through the test and scan the other words—*diminutive, imminent, abate, incredulous, mirth, palliation, semblance,* and *taciturn.* I know all of them. I studied so hard. But I'm never going to get through the rest of the questions in less than five minutes. I go back to the top of the page and try to use *sanguine* in a sentence. It doesn't matter that my hand is shaking, like I'm nervous even though I'm not, and that my writing is barely legible. I force myself to at least try to finish.

"That's time," Mr. Lee says. "Pencils down."

As soon as I drop mine, I remember the other definition for *sanguine—optimistic in a bad situation.*

Mr. Lee walks around the room and collects our tests. Most of mine is blank. It's bad. I did everything Ms. Curtis said to do and I took medicine. Everything is supposed to be better now. But I still got distracted and messed up, because my stomach hurt and I'm me. My ADHD wasn't even a problem. I didn't get distracted or stuck when I couldn't remember *sanguine.* I moved on and kept going. That part felt good. I don't want to lie to Mr. Lee, and I don't want to tell him that I didn't finish in front of everyone in class and that I need more time. They don't need to know. And I'm pretty sure more time won't help me anyway. Nothing will.

I try to pay attention and act like I did totally fine, because my problems are supposed to be gone, or at least smaller, now that I can focus. Except school feels exactly the same as always. Impossible.

When I get to math, I hold the balloon in one hand under my desk and take notes with the other, looking up at the board every few seconds. I remind myself to listen and write down what I need to remember. I squeeze, listen, and write over and over, until I fall into a rhythm. I'm so focused on taking notes that I don't notice the bell ring or everyone start to pack up and leave. When I'm finished copying everything into my note-book, I realize I'm alone, except for Ms. Pumi. I grab my back-pack and walk down the mostly deserted hall toward science.

I'm not hungry for lunch, like Mom said, but I have to find a way to eat, because I need energy for chess if I want to win today.

Dylan is at our table again with Red. But this time it doesn't feel like a bad thing, because when I sit down, he pulls a chess book out of his backpack, slides it over to me, and says, "You can keep it for as long as you want."

I look down at the cover. "This is perfect. Thanks." I grin.

He smiles back at me, showing off both dimples. He's so cute. "Let me know if you want to, um, talk strategies."

"K." I nod and look away, trying to act chill and, like, whatever, since I don't want to make it obvious to anyone, especially not to Dylan or Red, that on the inside I'm jumping up and down because he remembered.

I eat part of my lunch, make it through my next few classes, and by the time I get to chess, my stomach and head both feel better.

I'm playing white, which is good news for me, but I'm paired against Sanam, which is horrible because she's hard to beat.

The whole time we're sitting across from each other, waiting for practice to start, I want to tell Sanam that I think I failed my English test and that I probably won't be allowed to come to chess after today, unless I can find some magical way to fix my grade. But I don't say anything. Not now. I need to block it out and focus on playing my best.

I'm back in the chess tunnel, where it's quiet and safe. By the time we get to the endgame, Sanam moves her black king up one square on the diagonal, giving me a clear path to promotion. My pawn is only a few squares away from turning into a big, powerful queen! It's not the huge risk Dylan was talking about, but winning will help me turn things around. I'll be one step closer to proving to Mr. Lee that I belong in the advanced group at camp—if I still get to go to camp.

I take a sip of water and look around the board, laser focused in search of enemy pawns. Sanam has one on a5, but it can't move backward to capture me, so I'm good. This is it. I've got this. I'm about to crush this game and win! I slide my piece up one square and tap the clock.

Sanam picks up her king and moves it right back to where it came from, knocking out my soon-to-be-promoted pawn.

NO! UGH! What's wrong with me? I know the king can move in any direction. I was so focused on the stupid pawns that I completely forgot to notice everything else that was happening around me. And now all I want to do is rewind, look at the whole board, and make a different choice so I can win.

Sanam and I shake hands. But neither of us says good game, because it wasn't. I lost and she won, because I was distracted. The only good part is that we don't have to pretend everything is fine when it's not.

Mr. Lee stops me on my way out of practice. "Can you come by tomorrow before first period? I'd like to check in with you about your test."

I think about asking if we can talk now, but I don't want anyone else to hear what Mr. Lee is going to say to me and

I guess I don't actually want to hear my grade, because as soon as he says it out loud or writes it down on the top of my test, it will be real, so I nod and walk down the hall into the bathroom.

When the bell rings, everyone rushes out to dismissal. I wait a few minutes until the hallway is quiet and almost empty before I walk outside into the crisp air.

Red is sitting on our bench in the courtyard, waiting for me. "Sorry. My mom's late—again," he says. "It's her new thing."

"That's annoying," I say. "We should totally watch that Bobby Fischer movie on Friday." It's the first thing that pops into my head.

"Can't. I have plans."

"Really? What are you doing?" I ask.

"Going downtown after school with Quinn and a bunch of other chess peeps. I don't know what time that will be over, so . . ." He says it like it's no big deal that he made a whole group plan without me.

"Since when do you hang out with Quinn?"

"It's like a pre-tournament thing for the top twelve. She organized it. I didn't think you'd want to come, since you're, um, not anymore."

"I do." My words taste as desperate as they sound.

"Oh. Really? I mean, I guess you can, if you want to. It's a free country."

My neck feels hot, and I really hope I'm not turning red, because I don't want him to know how much it hurts. Everything I'm feeling and thinking is spinning around inside me like a tornado, threatening to come pouring out. And I can't let that happen. "So, are we not doing movie night anymore?" I try to sound chill and totally relaxed, like it's cool with me either way.

"It's kind of tired. Don't you think?"

"Not really," I say.

"Well, I do, so yeah, I think we shouldn't do it anymore." I keep waiting for him to realize how mean he sounds and take it back, but he doesn't. And it feels like I'm the only one who even cares if we're best friends.

"What's your problem?" I ask.

"Nothing," he says.

"That's such a lie. Just tell me."

"Why? So you can go around blurting it out to everyone in the entire school? No thanks, I'm good."

"I won't. I swear."

"I just don't believe you," he says. "You can't be different."

"But you said—"

"I changed my mind. I'm done. I can't deal with this anymore."

"You can't do that!" I shout before I can stop myself.

"Great meds. They're really working. Oh, wait, nope. You're already freaking out again."

"I'm not! Just give me one more chance. You have to!"

"Stop. You're embarrassing, and I'm sorry if that's mean or the wrong thing to say or whatever, but people don't just forget, Clea. They talk about you when you aren't there. Everyone thinks you're the reason we never play human chess in practice anymore. And I always make excuses for you, but I'm done. I can't deal with it." Before I have a chance to say anything else, Red's mom pulls up. He turns around and walks away from me.

I follow him to the car, because it's not like I have a choice. His mom is driving me home. I climb into the backseat and force myself to smile at Mrs. Levine. Then I look down at my glittery gold sneakers until we get to my house.

Mom and Henley aren't home yet. Hilda doesn't run over and start barking at me. I look around for her, but she isn't anywhere, so she must be with them, which is weird. I grab a snack, go up to my room, and start my homework. I use Ms. Curtis's strategies, because even though part of me feels like giving up, I know doing well in school is the only way I'm going to be able to stay on the team.

I'm about halfway done with history when there's a knock on my door.

"Come in," I say, even though I don't want to talk to anyone. Not even Henley.

Mom walks in and sits down next to me on my bed. "How did everything go today? With the medication?"

I shrug. "Not great."

"Tell me. What happened?"

"I felt different." I fidget with sand-filled balloon in my hands. "But it didn't actually help me in school. I had a stomachache during my English test, and I couldn't focus at all."

"I'm sorry." Mom rubs my shoulder. "Was your stomach upset all day?"

"Not really. Just in the morning."

She nods and makes a face like she feels sad for me. "Dr. Gold said that could happen at first."

"Seriously? The medicine I took to help me focus gave me a stomachache that made it impossible for me to focus? That's so stupid."

"I know it's frustrating. I'll call Dr. Gold to see if there's anything we can do to help with the discomfort. If it happens again tomorrow, please go to the nurse and have her call me," Mom says. "It's going to take time for you to get used to the medicine."

"How long?" I ask.

"I'm not sure."

"Great," I say back.

"Try to be patient. It will be okay."

"How?" My voice comes out too loud. "Things are supposed to be different, and I basically handed in a blank test and I yelled at Red. So, everything is exactly the same."

"We'll work out the right plan. I promise."

I don't believe her. Only I don't say that, because talking about how things are going to get better, when everything keeps getting worse, isn't helping. It makes me think that maybe Red is right and I can't change. And I'm afraid that no matter what I do or how hard I try I can't be a better friend to him or anyone and that school is always going to be like this for me.

"I know it's early, but will you take a break and eat dinner with us now?"

"I need to finish history and Spanish first."

"It's just—" Mom sighs. "Your sister had a tough day. We had an emergency speech appointment this afternoon, because Henley peed her pants in the middle of class. She couldn't ask to use the bathroom."

"Did anyone notice?" I ask, even though I'm pretty sure I already know the answer.

"What do you think?" Mom tilts her head.

I don't pause for a second to think. I stand up and walk out of my room, because even though I'm mad at Mom and Dad and Dr. Gold and Ms. Curtis and everyone who said they would help make things better for me when they can't, right now Henley *does* need me to be there for her and I don't want her to be alone.

I sit down at the kitchen table. Henley doesn't look up at me. She keeps her eyes on the plate in front her. I inch my chair closer to hers and wrap my arms around her. She folds into me. I run my fingers through her soft hair. Hilda is sprawled out under Henley's chair, like she knows something is wrong and her job is to stay as close as possible. "It's okay," I whisper in her ear.

She shakes her head.

"You're not the only one," I say, because when bad things happen to me, it always helps me to hear I'm not alone.

"I am."

"How do you know?"

"The Ellies said."

"They're wrong. Trust me. I'm older. I know," I say.

"You peed, too?" She looks up at me.

"No, but I've done a lot of embarrassing things that made me wish I were someone else." Henley shuts her eyes, drops her head, and leans into me. "The important thing is that you feel like you can ask for what you need, so it doesn't keep happening." As soon as I say it, I know it's true. I just wish I knew what to ask for to make things better for myself.

She looks up at me like she's thinking about what I just said. "I'll try." She nods. "It's really hard."

"I know." I pull her closer. "I'm proud of you for trying to do things that are hard for you."

"Thanks," she says. "Me too."

"Want to watch a show in my room while I finish my homework? We can eat dinner upstairs."

She looks up at me and smiles. Then she shakes her head. "We can't." And points to Mom.

I'm about to say that I'll handle Mom, but I stop myself. "Try asking," I whisper to Henley, because even though I just want to make everything easier and do it for her, I know I'm hurting her when I do that.

Henley's big blue eyes widen, like she can't believe me, and

209

I can't really, either. But I nod. It's what I need to do, even if it's hard for me. I take her hand in mine and squeeze, because I want her to know she's not alone, even if she has to do it herself.

"Can we please—" She looks at the floor. "Please." She squeezes my hand back. Mom takes a deep breath, like she's trying not to interrupt. "Can we finish dinner in Clea's room?"

Mom grins at Henley. "Of course. I'm glad you asked."

Henley smiles back.

Mom looks at me, and I can tell she's proud that I helped in a different, more important way—in the way that Henley actually needs.

After Henley and Hilda go to sleep and I'm done with all my homework, I take out the chess book Dylan let me borrow, because I want to start reading about strategies that are going to help me impress Mr. Lee. There's a piece of scrap paper tucked into the first page, folded twice. I almost throw it away, but I open it up just in case, which is really good because it turns out that it's a note for me from Dylan.

I hope this book helps you make the top twelve. Text me if you want to talk tactics.

From,

Dylan

PS. You can do it. ☺

I re-read Dylan's note again, because I'm afraid that I read it too fast or wrong the first time, and maybe it's not actually as nice as I think. But it is. He also wrote down his number. I save it. But then I get nervous that I'm going to text him by accident and he'll know I like him, and I don't want to make it obvious how I feel, unless he definitely likes me back. But I can't stop thinking about the fact that his number is permanently saved in my phone. It feels big.

TWELVE.

I'M GETTING READY for school when my phone starts buzzing. I hope it's Red texting to say he's sorry and he actually wants to be friends again, but it's Sanam: Are we going downtown on Friday?

Do you think it's weird if I go? I write back. *Red sort of said it was.*

No way. He's being weird.

But it's just for the top twelve.

I think it's the whole team or like anyone who wants to hang out after school, she replies. + I didn't play last week, and I'm going . . . if you are?

Yes! Let's go together.

Done. PS. My mom can totes drive us.

☺ ☺ ☺

When I get to school, I go straight to Mr. Lee's room. My stomach aches, churning up my breakfast, as he shuffles through the stack of papers. I'm not going to think about what's coming next. I stay focused on Mr. Lee's secret T-shirt, which says *Into the Woods*, until he finds my test in the middle of the pile and puts it on the desk in front of me. There's a big blue F at the top of the page.

My throat goes from dry to feeling like it's closing up. It doesn't matter that I knew the grade was going to be bad. Being prepared doesn't make failing any easier. I need to say something to convince him I deserve another chance, or I won't be able to play chess. "I studied a lot. I swear. I knew all the answers, but I started taking medicine yesterday for, um—because I have ADHD. It really hurt my stomach, and before I knew it class was over and I didn't get a chance to finish. If I can just retake the test at lunch, I'll do a lot better. I know I will. My stomach doesn't hurt as much today." I hold my breath and cross my fingers, because even though I'm not sure I can actually do any better if he gives me another chance, I need to at least try.

213

Mr. Lee sits down in the chair next to me and folds his arms across his chest, like he's thinking hard about what I said. "I understand that you were in a difficult position. The problem for me is that you know if you don't feel well during class, you can tell me and go to the nurse, and then I can let you retake the test. And I know ADHD is new to you, but Ms. Curtis explained that you're allowed to have extra time if you ask. If you were feeling up to taking the test, all you had to do was tell me and I would have absolutely made sure you had enough time. That's one of your accommodations."

"I know I messed up." My voice sounds strained. "Please just give me one more chance."

Mr. Lee sighs. "I'm sorry—but I can't make an exception this time."

No! That's not fair. "What about chess?" I ask.

"You'll have to sit out and attend study hall until you get your grade back up to a C, but I know you will," he says. "The good news is you have a paper due Monday, which is worth as much as this test. And what I can do is read yours and give it back to you by the end of the school day. That way if you get a B or higher, you'll be able to pick up where you left off at practice on Tuesday. This is probably not what you want to hear, but missing the tournament will give you time over the weekend to hand in your best work. I know you can do an excellent job, and then you'll be right back to playing chess."

My chest tightens. There's no way I'm going to be able to think about my paper while the rest of the team is at the tournament working together to win. Nope. That's impossible. But I'm pretty sure nothing I say or do is going to change his mind, and I need Mr. Lee to read my paper right away, because I want to be at practice on Tuesday and show him I belong in the top twelve. "Okay," I say.

"I look forward to reading your essay." He picks up my test and walks back over to his desk.

The hallway is hot and crowded with happy, smiling people who didn't fail their English tests. I try not to cry, but everything looks blurry and a few tears trickle down my cheeks. I brush them away as fast as I can. Red is standing by his locker. For a second, I almost forget we're not best friends. But when he sees me, his eyes drop to the floor and he turns away, and then I remember we're not even people who say, "Hey, what's up?" We're nothing.

Red starts talking to Vivi and smiling, like it's a regular day for him and he doesn't even care or notice or miss me at all. He's happy he doesn't have to deal with me anymore.

Everything I'm thinking and feeling is building up inside

of me, and if I don't walk faster, it's all going to pour out, and I can't let that happen, so I cover my mouth, holding my words in, and walk past him, down the long hall toward homeroom.

There are a few people in class when I get there. I sit in the front row by the window. I'm itchy under my thin wool sweater. I try to think about anything other than Red and English and how badly I messed everything up so I can breathe and be fine, but it feels like my brain is stuck replaying all the things I did wrong on a loop. It's impossible to switch to a different channel. I close my eyes and force myself to focus on something happy and easy—like Christmas. I think about our tree with its sparkling lights and huge white snowflake ornaments that look like shimmering pizzelles, and how Henley's face lights up when she watches the nutcracker turn into a prince, until I can breathe.

That's when I realize—I stayed totally calm and in control. And even though it was only one time, I didn't blurt out everything I was thinking, which means I can do it again. I'm pretty sure if I practice, it will get easier to be like that all the time.

I'm a few minutes early to science, so there's no one in the lab when I get there, which is fine by me. I stare out the window, watching the leaves and clouds. The next thing I know,

Sanam walks in and plops down at our table, dropping her bag and shoulders in one huff. I'm not sure I've ever seen her look like this—defeated and small.

"I hate today," she says.

"What happened?" I ask.

"I'm never moving to France or Canada or St. Barts or any place where people speak French, so I don't get the point of learning it." She slams her test down on the table so I can see the grade: C.

"I got everything right. I just—I can finally spell in English, most of the time, and now—" Her eyes look glossy. She shakes her head and takes a deep breath, like she's pushing all the sadness back inside.

"I'm sorry," I say, because even though I'd definitely trade my F for her C, I get how she feels, like she wants one thing to not be hard. "If it makes you feel better, I failed my English test."

"Wait. I thought—" She looks confused. "Did you not end up taking medicine?"

"I did, but—it's not, like, fixing me. It really hurt my stomach yesterday. That was basically the only thing I could think about during the test. And now I can't be on the team until I get my grade up."

"What? Not okay!" She sounds mad. "Fact: You just found

217

out you have ADHD. You're doing everything they've told you to do and they're still taking chess away." It feels good to hear Sanam say it's not what I deserve.

"Well, not everything," I say. "I didn't ask for extra time. But that's because it wasn't going to help, and it's embarrassing."

"You know extra time isn't just an ADHD thing, right? I mean, I get more time if I need it, and sometimes I do, especially if there's a lot of reading and writing, because it *does* help—a lot. I know it feels like a big deal, but it's really not."

I think about what she said. "I guess I never notice when other people ask for more time."

"Exactly," she says.

"What are you going to do about French?" I ask.

"I'm going to suck it up and talk to Ms. Curtis and come up with a plan for the next test, aka what I always do." She rolls her eyes. "Plus, I lied about not wanting to live in *tres chic* French-speaking places. I really love croissants."

"I think I need to talk to Ms. Curtis."

"You should. It helps."

"I'm sick of everything being hard," I say.

"I know! Like right now, even though I'm annoyed about getting a C, it's mostly because I should have asked for help before the test. I just didn't feel like being me this week. But I know what I need to do to get an A. You will, too. Trust me."

I shake my head. "I'm not good at school or smart."

"You don't really know that," she says. "I think that's the kind of thing that changes. Like right now, I'm the worst at French, but I'm good at everything else. And I wasn't always. I used to be bad at school, because I couldn't read. So maybe I can be good at French, too. I mean, considering that you didn't even know you had ADHD until, like, five seconds ago, I'm pretty sure you have no clue what you're good at."

"That's true," I say.

"The only way it won't work out for you is if you give up, so maybe don't do that."

"I definitely won't."

"Okay. Good."

"I hate that I'm missing two practices and a tourney," I say.

"Me too," she says. "But I'll text you live updates. It will be like you're there. Plus, we're going downtown with the team on Friday."

"I can't," I say.

"You have to. Everyone thinks you're going. It will be way worse if you don't show up."

"I know you're right. But also—Red is mad at me, so I don't want to make it awkward for you, because, you know—of the secret."

"He'll probably be over it by then."

I really hope she's right.

"We'll make it fun. I promise."

She holds out her pinky. I wrap my little finger around hers, squeezing tight. It feels like we're in on something together.

I don't have anyone to sit with at lunch, because Sanam has her tutor and Dylan is with Red, who hates me. Even if everything were fine with Red and he were missing lunch for some random reason, I would never sit with just Dylan in the cafeteria, unless I wanted everyone in the entire grade to know I like him, which I don't, so I go to the library between stacks of books. Even though I'm not hungry, I take out my PB&J, because I need energy to get through the rest of the day. The hardest part about eating after I take my medicine is the first bite. But I figured out that if I put the food up to my mouth and make myself try to eat, then it gets easier, because my body is actually hungry. It's just that my brain is busy with other things. Once I start eating, I have no problem finishing my sandwich, banana, and all my cherry-flavored seltzer.

When it's time for practice, the rest of the team walks past the library and over to the multipurpose room. I stay where I am for study hall. I try to use my time not playing chess to work on the outline for my English paper, but it's hard to think about anything other than what I'm missing at practice.

After the bell rings at the end of the day, I go to Ms. Curtis's office.

"Clea." She smiles when she sees me. "How can I help you?"

"I got an F on my English test, and I know you can't say I'm stupid, because you're a teacher and that's not allowed or whatever, but that's how I feel—like an idiot. I can't keep getting Fs, because then I won't be able to play chess, and it's the only thing I want to do, so I need you to help me not fail."

"I want you to listen to me very carefully, Clea." Ms. Curtis's voice is soft and calm, like always. "When I look at you, I see a hardworking student who is capable and talented, who I know can excel in every subject. And I know that because you're giving school everything you've got, even though it's hard and frustrating and it feels unfair."

"Then why isn't it working?"

"It will," she says. "ADHD is part of who you are and everything you do. It's how you process the world around you. It's going to take time to figure out how to manage your symptoms and make sure they're not getting in your way, and I know how hard that must be when you want everything to be fixed right now, but I think you're putting a lot of pressure on yourself—"

"I'm not!" I don't let her finish. "I got an F on my English test. That's really bad no matter how you look at it. I need to stop messing up."

"This is the time to mess up. That's how you're going to learn what you need to be your best, strongest self. Don't be afraid of failing. It's an opportunity," she says. "I think it would really help if you used your extra time during tests, even if you don't end up needing it. That way you won't feel rushed, and you can stay focused on finishing, instead of panicking about not getting to all the questions."

"I want to be able to do that," I say, because I know I have to ask for the things I need, like Sanam said. "I'm pretty sure I can ask my teachers, but I don't think I can do it in front of everyone in my classes. Maybe eventually. But that feels too hard right now."

"That makes sense," Ms. Curtis says. "One approach might be to remind your teacher at the beginning of the period before the test starts that you'll need extra time and sort out the logistics in advance. That way you have the option, but you don't have to feel the pressure to advocate for yourself in front of everyone while you're focused on finishing your work."

I think about her idea for a few seconds. "I'm pretty sure that would help."

"Good." She writes something in her notebook. "I know it might be hard for you to see it this way right now, especially because you're missing chess, but if you'd done better on your test, you might not have realized what you need in order to be successful."

I know she's right. "I think it might be better for me to take my tests in a quiet room. Maybe just for a little while or on days I'm feeling really distracted."

"Great idea." Ms. Curtis writes that down, too. "You can always come to the learning center during tests and quizzes, and I'll let your teachers know about the additional accommodation."

"Thank you," I say, because I'm pretty sure it's going to help.

"It's important for you to remember that what you need is going to change as you learn to manage your symptoms. Each day will be a little different."

"Is that a thing?" I ask. "Because I can kind of tell that some days are worse."

"Definitely. That's true for people without ADHD, too. Some days we're more distracted than others."

"Oh, yeah, duh," I say. "That makes sense."

"I'm very impressed that you came to see me today. It shows a lot of initiative, and I'm confident that if you continue to speak up and ask for the help you need, you'll grow a lot from this experience."

Thanks to Ms. Curtis, getting an F doesn't feel that bad anymore. It's a chance to turn everything around.

I sprint outside and over to the pickup line, because even though I know I did the right thing by going to see Ms. Curtis, I still feel bad that I kept Mom waiting. Only, when I get outside and see Red's car out front, I freeze. I completely forgot that Red's mom was picking me up today. I force myself to keep walking. I need to get in the car and act like everything is totally fine and we're best friends, the way we were

224

before this year started, because that's what I want more than anything.

"Everything okay?" Mrs. Levine asks as soon as I open the door and slide into the backseat.

"I'm sorry I'm late." I look at her in the mirror.

"It's okay," she says.

"What she really means is you're rude, and now she's late for her next appointment." Red doesn't turn around to look at me.

"That's not what I mean. It really is okay, Clea," Mrs. Levine says. "There are snacks, if you're hungry."

"Thank you."

Red turns up the music, even though it's funk, which he hates, and opens the window, like he doesn't even want to breathe the same air as me. Cold wind whips against my face.

When I get home, Mom and Henley are still out, so I let Hilda run around in our backyard for a few minutes, and then I make a snack—apple, banana, and peanut butter. My stomach is growling, and I can tell I'm hungry, even if my brain is busy thinking about homework and how mad Mom is going to be that I got an F on my English test.

I eat and work on science at the kitchen table. It's quiet,

except for the wind rustling the big tree by the window. When I look up again, Mom is standing in front of me holding her phone up to her ear with one hand. She has a box of freshly baked snickerdoodle cookies in the other. One of Henley's cartoons is playing in the family room. I didn't hear the garage door open and close or Henley run in or anyone take off their shoes and coats. I keep waiting for Mom to hang up so I can tell her about my test, and she can tell me how upset and disappointed she is in me.

"I just got home. I'm with Clea now," she says into the phone, and then hands it to me. "Dad wants to talk to you."

"Hi, Dad." My voice is soft. I sound more like Henley than like me.

"Ms. Curtis just called to tell us you had a tough day," Dad says. "I'm sorry, kiddo. I know it doesn't feel like it right now, but you can turn things around."

"What if I can't?" I ask.

He pauses, like he's thinking. "You'll get back up and try again. It's not like before. We know what's going on now, and you have a lot of people rooting for you. All you have to do is ask for help."

"Okay," I say, because I know he's right, and it's different now. I'm not alone.

226

"Just keep working hard. I love you."

"I will. I love you, too." I hang up and put the phone down on the counter.

Mom wraps her arms all the way around me, holding on as tight as she can, like she's afraid if she lets go, I might crumble, and I guess I'm sort of scared of that, too.

I lean into her and rest my head on her shoulder, and she scratches my back, drawing circles and hearts and all the letters in my name, until the alarm on my phone beeps. I switch it off.

Mom tucks my hair behind my ear.

"So, you know I got an F?" I ask.

She nods. "I also know that you went to Ms. Curtis to ask her for help after school. I'm very impressed."

"You are? Are you sure? I mean, I failed."

"No, you didn't," she says. "You showed us that you're not going to give up."

"I'm already missing two practices and a tournament. I don't want to miss anything else. And I know you're probably happy about that, but I'm not."

"That's not true," she says. "If I'm being honest, I want you to have a break from trying to do everything all at once, but—"

227

"I don't want a break." My voice sounds strained.

"I know," Mom says. "What I was going to say is that it's hard to learn to balance priorities at every age, and even though I hate watching you struggle and all I want to do is make things easier for you, I know the best way for you to learn how to juggle the things that are important to you is to practice."

"You don't have to worry. I can deal with things being hard," I say. "I'm kind of used to it."

"Well, I'm very proud of you for not giving up on chess and fighting for what you want. That takes real perseverance."

"Thanks," I say, because I know she's right. That's something I've learned from having ADHD. "Okay, so, I really don't get why you're not freaking out about my grade."

"Because I believe in you. I know you're capable of doing well in everything you set your mind to. But it's going to take time for you to get there. I'm learning to adjust and trying to put myself in your position so I can support you."

"Thanks," I say. "It helps a lot."

"I'm glad. That's all I want to do."

"Ms. Curtis told me that what I need is going to keep changing," I say, in case Mom doesn't know about that part.

"Then I'll have to keep adapting," Mom says. "We all will."

"I think we'll get better at it the more we do it."

"Me too," she says. "How was your stomach today?"

"A lot better."

"Good. I spoke with Dr. Gold earlier and she thought your stomachache might go away, but if it starts hurting again at any point, I want you to tell me."

"Okay. I will," I say. "Oh, I forgot to ask—can I go downtown with the chess team on Friday after school? Sanam's mom can drive us."

"Of course," Mom says. "I'll give her a call to say thank you."

"Thanks," I say.

"So what do you think? Should we eat some of these cookies?" Mom asks.

"Duh," I say. "But we should probably let Henley in on our secret party."

Mom rubs my back. "You're a good big sister."

"Henley!" I shout. "We're having cookies before dinner."

"YES!" she shrieks and runs into the kitchen, like she's ready to celebrate. And I am, too. It feels like everything is about to get better.

THIRTEEN.

ON FRIDAY, I wake up early and try to look extra pretty, because even though I'm nervous to go downtown with the team and Red, now that we're not friends anymore, I'm excited to hang out with Sanam and maybe Dylan, too.

School is basically the same—still bad. Maybe a little worse actually, because ever since I missed practice, people on the team whisper about me when I walk by.

At lunch, I go to the library. I pick an empty table as far away from the librarian's desk as possible, because even though it's supposed to be quiet, she whispers and rustles papers, which bothers me. And I've decided that from now on, I'm going to do everything I can to help myself, like Sanam and Ms. Curtis said I should.

I open my outline and am about to start working on my paper when Dylan sits down across from me.

"Hey," he whispers.

"Hey." I look up at him. His hair is shorter and a little less floppy than usual. He looks even cuter with a new cut, because his eyes aren't hidden. They're big and blue and looking back at me. My stomach flips.

"What do you think of the chess book?" he asks.

"I'm only on chapter three."

"Oh. Okay. No pressure. If you're not into it, it's cool."

"I am," I say quickly.

"You don't have to be."

"I know. But I like that it's a different way to look at chess. It's just that I'm doing this new thing where I read everything twice so I don't miss as much." I fiddle with the rubbery part of my pencil. I want to tell him the truth. "Because I have ADHD. I found out last week, so I'm trying to follow all the suggestions."

"That must be hard," he says.

"Yeah," I tell him. "But it's good, too. Or at least I think it might be soon."

"I bet it helps to know what's actually going on."

"Yeah," I say. "It does."

"Cool." He pushes back his hair. "Are you going downtown tonight?"

I nod. "But I feel weird, because it's a team thing, and I'm not really—I got a bad grade on a test, so I can't go to the tournament or practice until Tuesday or maybe longer, if I don't get at least a B on this paper." I look down at my notebook.

"That's why you weren't at chess," he says, like maybe he thought there was another reason. I should ask him what people are saying, but I don't think I want to know.

"It's going to take time for me to learn how to deal with having ADHD."

"That makes sense," Dylan says.

"There's probably no way I'm going to make the top twelve before camp."

"You never know." He shrugs. "It could still happen. Just play your best. That's all you can do."

"Thanks," I say. "I will."

"You're really good. I know I said you weren't, but I was just—"

"A jerk," I fill in.

"Pretty much. I'm sorry. It wasn't cool at all. I was jealous—of you and Red."

"Me too," I say. "And BTW, I would never quit chess no matter what you or anyone else says."

"Good." He smiles at me.

I smile back. "I should give you my number, so when I text you all my amazing chess ideas you'll know who it is."

"You should." He passes his phone to me under the table.

I save my number and give it back to him. Only this time, when I hand him his phone, our fingers touch. His are warm and soft and I'm pretty sure he keeps his fingers next to mine for a few extra seconds, like maybe he doesn't want to let go, either.

When I get to science, Sanam and I collect all the materials we need for our crystallization lab. We both put on gloves and goggles. I read the directions out loud twice and then we get to work, dividing up the tasks, like the lab is a choreographed dance we know by heart. I mix the alum into a beaker with hot water, stir, and repeat, until the solution is saturated, while Sanam uses string to tie pipe cleaners onto wood craft sticks.

We're quiet, concentrating on our jobs, until everything is set up and ready to go. "You were right about talking to Ms. Curtis," I say. "It helped."

233

"I knew it! That's awesome." She picks up the stirrer and rests it on top of the jar so the pipe cleaner dangles inside, but doesn't touch the glass. Then I pour in the solution.

"In chess, Quinn said you're not friends with Red anymore, because you want to be boyfriend-girlfriend and he doesn't." She sounds nervous. "I don't care if you like him. We can like the same boy. That's cool with me, but when I asked you, you said you didn't and I just want to know."

I want to say the truth, but I'm scared if I tell her that what happened at the raffle wasn't a one-time thing and I actually blurt stuff out all the time, she won't want to be my friend, either. Sanam and I are real friends now, who tell each other secrets, and I don't want that to change. She trusted me and I know I can trust her back. "Red and I aren't friends anymore. But I never liked him like that. I would have told you if I did."

"Oh. Okay," she says, like now she's really confused. "What happened?"

"We—" I stop myself and take a deep breath. "I lose it sometimes. I say things out loud that I really don't mean to."

"Like what happened at the raffle?"

I nod. "The medicine helps, but I need to practice and get

better at staying calm. And Red doesn't want to be friends anymore, because I'm embarrassing and he's sick of me. I don't really blame him. I am, too. That's why I didn't tell you."

"Wait, really? I mean, I get that you spilled his family secrets and that was bad, but still—"

"I don't think it was because I did it once. It was more like a lot of the same mistake that added up into something bigger that I can't take back now even though I really wish I could."

"That stinks," she says. "Do you think you can change?"

"I want to."

"I bet you will. I'm pretty sure that's how it works. You can make most things happen if you keep trying."

"I really hope you're right," I say, because I need that to be true.

After we finish setting up the sugar and salt solutions, I realize I haven't told anyone about my crush, which is especially weird for me, since I usually can't keep things like that to myself. Plus, I'm pretty sure a crush isn't official until you tell someone, and I want Sanam to know. So I lean in and whisper, "I like Dylan."

"OMG! Really?" Her eyes get wide. "I love it! We could be best friends going out with best friends!"

* * *

After school, Sanam's mom picks us up. I love how their car smells new, like leather and soap, and how the backseat isn't covered in crumbs or sticky fingerprints or toys. It makes me feel grown-up and important.

When we get downtown, her mom drops us off in front of The Hideout, which is sort of like a coffee shop that sells fancy pastries and has big comfy chairs and a fireplace. "I'll be here at five to pick you girls up," she says. "Have fun."

"Thank you," we both reply at the exact same time.

I follow Sanam out of the car. My heart starts beating so fast it hurts. "I'm not ready to go in yet." My voice is soft.

"Let's take a lap." She turns away from The Hideout.

Even though it's cold, the air feels good as we walk in a loop past the stores in the center of town. "I haven't really seen Red since our fight and I don't know what it's going to be like now that we're not friends," I say.

"I get why you're nervous, but I mean, just because you're not best friends anymore doesn't mean you have to be rude to each other."

"True," I say.

"Maybe act normal and see how that goes."

"But what if he ignores me?"

"Then we'll leave and get hot chocolate at Sweet Sadie's. We don't need the team to have fun."

"Okay," I say. "Thanks."

"We probably need a secret signal," she says. "That way the other person will know if we want to leave."

"How about a peace sign? Like peace, we're out of here."

"Yes, that's perfect," she says. "Do you want to take another lap?"

I shake my head. "I'm ready." I open the door, and we walk into The Hideout.

Dylan and Red are sitting in front of the fireplace.

Sanam looks at me, like she's waiting for me to go first. I'd rather get hot chocolate and avoid Red for a few more minutes, but I know it's better to say hi while Quinn isn't here to make everything worse. I take a deep breath and walk over to them. Sanam stays right by my side. She slides into the empty seat by Red, and I sit next to Dylan. I'm nervous and sweating a little. I hope he can't tell.

"Big turnout," Sanam says.

Red smiles. "Two dudes. Lots of team spirit."

"Where is everyone?" I ask and act like everything is totally fine and normal.

"We were trying to figure that out while you two were walking around outside." Dylan looks right at me.

"Busted," I say.

"What were you doing out there anyway?" he asks.

"Talking about—girl stuff," Sanam jumps in.

"Oh," he says. "That's cool."

We're all quiet for a few seconds. No one says anything.

"I need a refill. Want one?" Red looks at Sanam and then at Dylan. He doesn't look at me. It's like I'm not even here. My heart sinks.

"Dude, I'll help," Dylan says to Red.

Once the boys are gone, Sanam leans in and whispers, "You okay?"

I want to say not really and flash her the peace sign, but I grip the edge of my chair and take a deep breath, because I know if I say that, she'll get up and leave, and I don't want Sanam to miss out on having fun with Red because of me. I want to be the kind of friend who makes things better, not worse. "Yeah. I'm okay," I say. "Thanks for asking."

When Dylan and Red get back, they're each holding two hot chocolates.

Dylan hands one to me. "I didn't know if you wanted whipped cream, but I, um, got it for you because it's way better than no whipped cream."

"Thanks," I say. "You made the right choice."

"Phew." He grins.

When I look up again, Quinn is walking over to us with a bunch of other girls from the team. She's wearing a cropped sweatshirt that says, *Okay, But First Coffee,* like she's so adult and actually drinks anything other than sugary frozen cappuccinos, when she obviously doesn't. "Why are *you* here?" She looks down at me. "I'm not trying to be rude, but you got kicked out of chess because you're stupid, remember? So, bye." She waves me away.

A few of the girls laugh.

I can't let her talk to me like I'm dumb and I don't matter. "You wish," I say. "I'll be there on Tuesday."

"So watch out," Sanam says, backing me up.

"Ooh. I'm scared." Quinn rolls her eyes.

"Well, you should be," Sanam says. "Clea will take your spot if you don't step up your game."

"Never happening," Quinn says.

239

"Keep losing like you have been, and it's going to happen at the next tournament."

"I—"

"Save your excuses for someone who cares."

Quinn doesn't say anything else. She turns around and walks away, into the bathroom. And even though I know we won that round and Quinn is the one who's wrong, I wish everything she said about me didn't hurt so much.

Sanam glances over to check on me, like she knows to be worried. But I don't want her to be. I want her to have fun with Red, even if he hasn't acknowledged my presence once since we got here. I give Sanam a look that says I'm totes fine and she should go back to flirting.

"Are you okay?" Dylan whispers to me.

I shrug.

"So . . . not really?"

"I wish that what Quinn said didn't bother me."

"For the record, she's wrong," he says. "But I get how you feel."

"Doubt it," I say. "You're so good at chess, and you know it."

"I'm good for our grade, but my brother is always ragging on me about my openings and I don't even know—other random parts of my game. He acts like there's only one way to be good at chess. And when he says things enough times and in a certain way, they start to sound true."

"That stinks," I say. "Just because he's better than you, doesn't mean he's always right about chess."

"That's why I stopped playing with him. He was making me hate the game. And I'm pretty sure that's another reason I was rude to you and other people on the team."

"I didn't know that," I say. "I'm really glad you don't play with him anymore."

"Yeah. Me too. I needed to stand up for myself," he says. "I guess what I'm saying is sometimes when people are mean, they're also wrong, and you have to find a way to block them out. Quinn is wrong about you. You're smart and the team needs you. I should know—you crushed me."

"Oh, yeah," I say. "I forgot about that."

"I didn't," he says.

"Well, you got blindsided. That's hard to forget."

"Ouch," he says. "But true."

"Thanks for saying I'm smart and good at chess."

"You are," he says. "Believe it."

"I'm really trying to."

I end up staying at the hangout the entire time, talking to

Dylan, and I never have to use the secret peace signal. Right before it's time to go home, Sanam and I get extra hot chocolate to celebrate.

When I get home, Dad isn't on the couch or in his office or upstairs in my parents' room. Mom said he got delayed until tomorrow because of weather, which makes no sense, since it's not raining or anything, but apparently I'm wrong, because when I look online, it turns out that all the planes coming into Logan are delayed or canceled due to a "low ceiling," whatever that means.

I go up to my room and read the chess book Dylan gave me. I almost finish the whole thing, because I can't put it down. All of a sudden, reading feels exactly like playing chess. I didn't realize until now that hyper focus can happen other times, too! Basically whenever I'm doing something I love. I really like being able to block out all the bad things and think about something that makes me happy. It feels a little like magic.

The best part about Dylan's book is that it reminds me about moves that I sort of forgot existed, like castling on the queen's side, which is not anything crazy or weird or even new for me, but it's good to remember. I usually castle king-side, moving the king to the right next to the rook. Once the pieces are side by side, they swap places, so the rook can protect the king. If you want to castle queen-side you have to get the queen out of the way and then move the king to the left.

The whole time I'm reading my brain is spinning and whipping up moves I can use to impress Mr. Lee once I'm back on the team.

FOURTEEN.

I WANT TO cry when I hear my phone beep, buzz, and jingle at 8:15 a.m. I hit snooze. I need a few more minutes of sleep. I can't get up yet. It's so cozy and comfy. I'm barely awake, but I know I have to pull myself out of bed and leave my room, before I can't help but get back under the layers of fluffy blankets. I need a good grade on my paper so I can be back on the chess team and make the top twelve before camp.

Last night, after I read most of Dylan's chess book, I looked over the schedule Ms. Curtis helped me make for my paper with achievable goals and rewards.

CLEA'S HOMEWORK SCHEDULE AND LIST OF AWESOME REWARDS:

SATURDAY:

1. **FINISH OUTLINE:** PLAY FIFTEEN MINUTES OF CHESS PUZZLES.
2. **WRITE A THESIS STATEMENT AND FIND THREE SUPPORTING PIECES OF EVIDENCE:** WATCH ONE EPISODE OF <u>BEWITCHED</u>.
3. **WRITE THREE SUPPORTING PARAGRAPHS:** HANG OUT WITH HENLEY FOR TWENTY MINUTES.
4. **FINISH CONCLUSION:** TEXT OR CALL SANAM FOR TEN MINUTES.
5. **STUDY FOR SPANISH QUIZ:** FREEDOM FOR THE REST OF THE NIGHT!

SUNDAY:

6. **ASK MOM AND DAD TO READ MY PAPER AND THEN REVISE:** PRACTICE CHESS PUZZLES FOR TEN MINUTES.
7. **REVISE MORE AND FINISH:** EAT DESSERT!
8. **FINISH MATH AND HISTORY HOMEWORK:** DO WHATEVER YOU WANT/HAVE A DANCE PARTY, BECAUSE YOU'RE DONE WITH EVERYTHING!

The schedule is tight. I have to focus and complete every single thing on my list in a limited time frame, or I won't finish.

245

Waking up early isn't on the schedule. It's a cushion, a way to trick myself into feeling like I'm ahead. It's one of the things I need to do my best. That isn't something Ms. Curtis taught me. I figured that out on my own.

When I get downstairs, Henley is sitting next to Mom at the kitchen table. They're always up early tiptoeing around the house, even on weekends. Dad and I both like to sleep in whenever we have a chance. Henley has a blue marker in one hand and a waffle in the other. "Clea!" she shouts. There's sticky maple syrup all over her lips, like gloss that she put on by herself.

I smile at her.

"What are you doing up so early?" Mom asks.

"English paper."

She walks over and rubs my shoulder. "Want a waffle?"

"They have chocolate chips inside," Henley says.

"I don't have time for a big breakfast," I say.

"You have the whole weekend to finish your work. I'm confident you'll have enough time to get everything done. I don't want you to be so hard on yourself. You need to eat something now before you take your medicine," Mom says. "That's not up for discussion, and you can also bring a waffle or anything else you'd like up to your room."

"Okay," I say, because I know she's right. I figured out that I have a twenty-minute window before the medicine kicks in and makes me think I'm not that hungry. "A waffle sounds good." I pour myself a glass of juice and open a banana. I eat the whole thing, take my medicine, and sit down at the kitchen table.

"I want to help you with homework," Henley says.

"Not today." I smile at her.

"I can. I'm good at helping."

"I know, you are." I look at the clock. I want to be upstairs at my computer in ten minutes so that I'm ready to write my paper when the medicine starts working.

"So, yes?!" She stands up like she's ready to get to work.

"Not this time." I try as hard as I can to sound calm.

"Please. Please. Pretty please with sugar on top."

"No." The word comes out a little too loud.

"Clea, be nice." Mom says it like she hasn't heard all the times I've tried to be.

"I was," I snap. "I didn't do anything wrong."

"It's really hard for your sister to express herself. You need to be supportive. We all need to be. That's not optional."

"Well, writing an entire English paper due Monday and finishing all my other homework is really hard for *me*." My voice is loud and mad. "I'm barely going to have enough time to finish as it is."

"You need to calm down," Mom says. "She just wants to help with something."

"There's literally no way for Henley to help me. She's six!" The words fly out of my mouth before I can stop them.

"SIX AND THREE QUARTERS!!!" Henley shouts back at me. There are tears in her eyes.

"Do you see what you've done?" Mom puts a plate of food on the table in front of me and points to my sister. "Look."

Only I can't. The sound of her tiny chest heaving, choking between tears to find air, hurts me. I didn't mean to make her cry. She didn't do anything wrong. I take a deep breath and look at her. There are tears trickling down her face.

"I'm sorry," I say.

She crosses her arms over her body and looks at me like she never has before, like she hates me.

I take a deep breath. "It's not because you're younger that you can't help. I shouldn't have said that. It's not true."

"I already know," she says like it's so obvious to her. "It hurts when you yell. I don't like it."

"I know," I say. "I'll do a better job next time. I promise."

"Good," she says.

248

"You have to be responsible for your words," Mom says. "I don't want you to accidentally say something that you can't take back."

"You can't be serious right now! Don't you think I know that? That's why Red isn't my best friend anymore!"

"He isn't?" Mom asks.

I shake my head. "He isn't even my friend. We're basically strangers."

"I'm sorry to hear that. Did something happen?"

I can feel the tears building up behind my eyes. I've been trying so hard not to think about how much I miss Red or about all the stupid things I said by accident that I shouldn't have, that I wish I could take back now. "I blurted out secrets about his family in front of a lot of people, and even though I was trying to defend him, I ended up embarrassing him. It was really bad. And I do that kind of a lot. So now he doesn't want to know me."

Mom sighs. "I know you're not proud of what you said, but I think Red is having a really hard time right now, so whatever happened probably felt like a much bigger deal to him than it actually was, and maybe with a little more time, you can figure out a way to be friends again."

"I hope so," I say. "But I don't want to say anything I don't mean to ever again."

"That's a great goal. What can I do to help you?"

"I need to practice not saying everything I'm thinking so I can get used to staying calm, but it's hard when I'm upset. Whatever you do, don't tell me to calm down, because I'm already trying to do that and it's not working, so hearing you say it, like it's so easy, makes me more upset. What I really need is a reminder that I should take my time and think about what I want to say."

"I can do that." Mom rubs my shoulder.

"Thanks for listening," I say. "I know I'll get used to everything about ADHD. I already have. Some things are better. But it's hard. And it's going to take time and practice."

"It's okay if you mess up again," Henley says. "I'll still be your sister. But try hard not to, okay?"

I nod. "I will."

"You can do it," she says.

And I know she's right.

The garage door opens, and a minute later, Dad walks into the kitchen. "My three favorite people." He smiles at each of us. "What did I miss?"

"A lot!" Henley says. "We have problems."

We all laugh.

"Is there anything I can do to help solve your problems?" Dad asks Henley.

She puts her hand up to her chin like she's thinking hard. "Nothing for me."

"I really need you to read my English paper." I look at Mom and then at Dad. They both nod back at me. "I know you have a lot of work, but this is important to me. I need you to not just pretend like you're going to help and then get too busy. I can't make any major mistakes or I won't be allowed back on the chess team for—I don't even know how long."

Dad says, "I've done that to you a lot recently, and it's not fair. I'm sorry. You can show me as many drafts of your paper as you need to so that you feel great about what you hand in."

"Thank you," I say.

"I'm really glad you asked for help," he says.

"Me too."

"I have some good news. My work in California is on hold for now, so I won't need to travel for a few weeks."

"Yes!" Henley jumps out of her chair and runs over to Dad, hugging him as hard as she can.

Mom smiles.

And I do too.

When I get back up to my room, I decide to write about

the magic in *A Wrinkle in Time*, because I realize the best chance I have at writing a great paper is to pick a topic that interests me. I might as well take advantage of my hyper focus. It only takes me an hour to write my introductory paragraph and find three examples to support my thesis. After I finish reading over what I wrote, I'm confident that I'm off to a great start.

My phone starts dinging. It's a text from Sanam:

It's not the same without you. I wish you were here! ☺

I can't help but smile. It feels good to be missed. And even though texting Sanam wasn't supposed to be my first or second reward, I figure it's okay to switch that part around, as long as I stay on schedule with my paper.

Me too! I write back.

We're running late, so nothing chess related is even happening yet. But everyone is talking about you . . .

My heart stops. *What are they saying?* I ask, because this time I want to know. I can handle it, even if it's not nice or the truth. It doesn't matter what anyone else thinks. I know I'm a great chess player and I can get a good grade on my paper and turn things around in school.

That Dylan likes you and wants to be boyfriend-girlfriend for real!

SHUT UP?!

I swear! OMG!!!! It's major! she texts.

I was worried everyone was making fun of me.

I didn't even think about that!

That's definitely a good thing ☺, I write. *I just wanted you to know.*

I'm glad you told me, she writes back.

Me too.

I run around outside with Henley and Hilda for a few minutes, and then I get back to work on my paper.

It takes me almost three hours and a lot of playing with the squishy ball and pacing around my room to write my supporting paragraphs, but when I'm done, I think they're pretty good for a first draft. Instead of writing the conclusion and waiting until tomorrow to have Mom and Dad read through my paper, I realize it's probably better for me to have them read it now so I have all day tomorrow to revise. I'm still learning how to plan out my homework and manage my time, so I have to be flexible.

I print out two copies of my paper and walk downstairs.

My parents are in the family room watching *Casablanca*, which is this old black-and-white movie they love.

Mom pauses the movie when she sees me.

"I didn't write the conclusion yet, but could you maybe read what I have so far?"

"Yes. Let me get my glasses." Mom disappears into the kitchen.

"Could you grab a pen?" Dad asks her.

She comes back with both.

I hand them each a copy and then escape into the kitchen for a late lunch, because I'm hungry and I don't think it's a good idea for me to watch my parents write all over my paper. I go to text Sanam, because the tournament should be finishing up soon and I want to know if we won. That's when I remember my phone has been on do not disturb, and it turns out I missed a bunch of texts from her:

Everyone crushed the first round, including moi!

I lost round two ☹. PS. It would be way better if you were here.

Round three = draw for me.

Spoiler alert . . . We won!!!

BTW text me back soon, so I know you're okay/not annoyed.

I write back to Sanam immediately. ***SORRY! Phone was off. Def not annoyed ever/at all! You're the best at chess and updates and yay for winning. I'm sad I wasn't there, too.*** ☹

PHEW! Sanam writes back. It's almost Tuesday!

I can't wait, I tell her.

Ditto.

I finish my sandwich and an orange, and then I walk back into the family room, sit in the cushy chair across from my parents, and hold my breath.

Neither of them says anything at first. Dad looks down at the stapled pages and nods. "It's very interesting, and your thesis definitely works."

"Really?" I blurt out.

"You've done a great job making an argument and backing it up," Mom says. "I have some minor notes and one comment on the third example, but overall it's excellent."

"You don't have to sugarcoat it. I mean, if it's not good enough, I can start over," I say, because out of nowhere I'm scared they aren't telling me the whole truth, since they're worried about me.

"This is a wonderful draft, Clea." Mom's voice is steady. "You should be very proud."

255

Dad is nodding, like he agrees with everything Mom just said.

"Yes!" I jump up and down and hug Mom and then Dad.

I'm so excited that I go back upstairs to work on their edits and write my conclusion. It feels good to finally be on the right track.

FIFTEEN.

ON MONDAY, I wake up early to re-read my paper one last time with fresh eyes, and it's awesome! I can't wait to hand it in and get a good grade. I want this whole not-playing-chess situation to be over and old news. I pack a copy of my paper in my bag with the book Dylan let me borrow so I can give it back to him. The note he wrote me with his number is already tucked away in my desk drawer. I read it a few times this weekend whenever I started to get sad about missing the tournament. It made me feel better, and like I'm still on the team and a great chess player.

After I'm done getting ready for school, I have time to

practice chess puzzles, which is good news, because I need to keep my skills super sharp for Tuesday.

I set my alarm for twenty minutes without even thinking, like it's already an old habit, and I start playing. I'm thrown right into the middle of a game. I spot my move immediately and take out the enemy pawn with my queen, so there's only one space between my queen and my opponent's king. The enemy rook slides over to save his king. I don't fall for it. I slide my queen up two squares on the diagonal, take out another rook, and take back my direct access to the king! I practice my tactics until my phone starts beeping. Then I stop, pack the rest of my books in my bag, and go downstairs for breakfast.

At school, everyone is waiting inside because it's raining. I look around for Sanam, but I don't see her anywhere. That's when I realize she's with Red. They're pretty close together and she's smiling really big. I don't go over to them. I can't ruin this moment for her by showing up and making things awkward with Red.

"So, do you think that's a thing?" Dylan asks. I look up as soon as I hear his voice.

I'm not sure what Sanam would want me to say right now, and I don't want to make it obvious that she likes Red, unless I know he likes her back. I shrug. "Do you?"

"It definitely is," Dylan says.

"Cool." I smile.

We're both quiet for a few seconds, and I can't decide if it's cute or awkward that we're talking about other people liking each other, when I'm pretty sure we both like each other, too. I think about giving Dylan back his book, but it doesn't seem like the right time, and I guess I kind of like carrying something around that I know belongs to him, even if it does make my bag heavier.

"You know, Red and I aren't friends anymore," he says.

"Are you kidding?"

He shakes his head. "Nope. He got mad after we went downtown. I guess because I was talking to you, which is dumb, since the whole time we were hanging out, he was talking to Sanam, so it's kind of a double standard, you know?"

"Yeah," I say. "That's really not okay."

"There's all that stuff with his dad. And I get that he feels like being a jerk to someone, because he's mad. But it's not going to be me."

I nod, because I think Dylan is right, and it seems like that might be part of the reason Red got so mad and pushed me away, too. I'm starting to think it wasn't all my fault. It makes me sad for him and worried that he doesn't have a best friend to talk to about everything with his family.

"He's the one who told everyone that I, um, like you." Dylan's voice is so soft I almost miss it.

I can feel my face turn red. "I like you, too," I say before I can think about it and stop myself.

"But you didn't text me," he says.

"You didn't, either."

"True." He grins.

I smile back at him, and I can't stop smiling for the rest of the day.

"Disculpe," I say to Señora Campo when I get to Spanish class. She's standing at the board writing down our next assignment.

"¿Cómo puedo ayudarte?" She asks how she can help me.

Only I have no idea how to say what I need in Spanish. And even though I can always ask her how to say it in English—"Cómo se dice 'I need to go to the learning center during the quiz and also I need extra time'?"—I already feel weird asking and like maybe I'll be fine taking the quiz in class with everyone else. Only I know that's not true. Not yet. Maybe one day. And if I'm going to bother asking, I know Señora Campo would rather I try saying it in Spanish, even if I get all the words wrong. "¿Está bien si necesito voy a la learning center para el cuestionario y necesito extra tiempo?"

"Tiempo extra," Señora Campo corrects my phrasing of "extra time," and then she says, "¡Sí, por supuesto!" which means "Yes, of course!"

"Wait—" I say. "Sorry. I know it's better to speak in Spanish, but I, um, want to make sure I said everything right, because it's important."

"You were very clear," Señora Campo says. "It probably makes sense for you to head over to the learning center now and get started. I'm giving everyone twenty-five minutes to finish the quiz, but you can have until the end of the period." I keep waiting for Señora Campo to ask why I need to take my quiz in the other room, but she doesn't. Even though I know Ms. Curtis told all my teachers about the new accommodations, I guess I didn't realize until now that they're not a big deal to anyone, other than me.

"Thank you," I say. "I mean, gracias."

"De nada."

When I get to the learning center, there's another student in the corner of the room—a sixth grader who I recognize from when we played human chess. She glances up at me and then looks back at her paper. I pick a seat on the opposite side of the room and get right to work on the fill-in-the-blanks and short-answer questions. It's so much easier for me to stay focused in the quiet room. I get through the first two pages fast. The third page is harder, because it's a creative essay in Spanish, and it takes me kind of a while to think of an idea that I like. But I still manage to finish the entire test in twenty-five minutes!

I take my extra time to double-check all my answers, and I'm glad I do, because I find a few careless mistakes I shouldn't have made.

By the time I'm officially done, there are still fifteen minutes left in the period. I walk back down the hall to class, put my quiz in the pile on Señora Campo's desk, and sit down in one of the empty chairs. I don't notice if anyone starts whispering about me when I walk back into the room, but I don't care if they do, because for the first time all year, I got exactly what I needed and I know for sure I did my best.

I feel really great about my English paper when I hand it in, but I start to get nauseous during last period because I'm so nervous, and by the time I get to Mr. Lee's room to find out my grade, there's a strong possibility that I'm going to puke.

Mr. Lee smiles when I walk in, which means nothing. I'm pretty sure he grinned at me the day he gave me the F and took chess away.

I sit at one of the chairs in the front row.

"Give me a minute, Clea." He looks around his cluttered desk. "I have your paper here somewhere."

Breathe. I'm trying to think of a polite way to ask him to just tell me how I did already when he says, "Ah-ha. Got it." I hold my breath. Mr. Lee sits down and then puts my paper on the desk in front of me.

There's an A at the top of the page!

I pick up my essay and hold it closer to make sure it's real. It is! I take a deep breath and let out everything I've been holding inside. "Thank you! Thank you!" I say.

"Thank yourself. You're the one who made it happen. Keep up the great work," he says.

"I will," I say. "I promise."

"I'll see you at practice tomorrow."

I sprint over to the car, and as soon as I see Mom and Henley, I shout, "I did it! I got an A!"

"Duh! I already knew," Henley says.

"That's amazing, Clea. Well deserved." Mom reaches over and wraps her arms around me. "Wait, that means you're back on the team!" She says it like she's just putting it together now. "We need to celebrate!"

"Ice cream sundae party!" Henley shrieks. "With hot fudge and gummies!"

Mom looks at me.

"That's perfect," I say, and I mean it.

When we get home, I go straight up to my room and text Sanam, *I'm back on the team!!!*

YES! I was going to ask, but then I was like . . . don't do that.

Always ask.

Okay, cool. ☺ I will, she promises.

Wait—I can't believe I almost forgot. I have major news, I type. *I heard from "someone" aka a reliable source (you can probably guess who) that Red definitely likes you! It's official.*

OMG. OMG. OMG.

Best day ever, I write back.

Seriously!!!

I take out my planner and look at the very short list of things I have to do tonight. Even though I hated missing chess, Mom was right about having a break to catch up. It feels good to be ahead in school for once.

I'm about to start my homework for Wednesday when my phone buzzes again. I pick it up, because I think Sanam is writing something else about the Red situation, except it's Dylan. *OMG! We're texting! This is really happening.* It feels like a really big deal, since we were just talking about how texting equals liking each other. Also, his name looks so good in my phone and like it totally belongs there.

Did you read any more of the book?

Yes! I finished it, I write back, because I ended up carrying Dylan's chess book around in my bag all day and never gave it back to him. *Watch out. I'm ready to win big.*

Wait. Does that mean you'll be at practice tomorrow?

You know it, I text.

That's awesome!

I'm pumped. BTW thanks for letting me borrow the book.

No prob, he says. I feel bad for whoever gets paired up against you.

☺. *Same.*

"Clea! Henley!" Dad shouts. "Time for dinner!"

GTG. Dinner, Dylan texts.

Me too, I reply. *TTYL.*

When I get downstairs, not only has Mom set up the

coolest ice cream sundae bar ever with caramel sauce and cookie crumbles, my two all-time favorite toppings, but Dad surprises us with homemade pizza! I can tell Mom and Dad want tonight to be special for me. And it feels like everything is finally falling into place.

SIXTEEN.

I'M SO EXCITED for chess. It doesn't even bother me that the minute I walk into the room, Quinn starts whispering and pointing in my direction. I get that she's trying to make me feel like I shouldn't be here because I don't belong, but for once, I don't care what she thinks or says about me. I want to win, and I know I can.

Red is sitting alone near the door. He looks at me and I think maybe he's going to say something, but then he turns away. I walk across the room and over to Dylan. I get that sitting next to him is basically the equivalent of wearing a sign that says I want to be boyfriend-girlfriend, but I do. And even though I know he likes me, too, I'm still nervous. "Welcome back," he says when he sees me.

"Thanks!" I reach into my bag, take out his chess book, and hand it to him.

He flips through the pages. "I feel like I'm going to regret giving this to you."

"Only if you have to play against me."

"I was already scared of that."

"For good reason," I say.

He smiles.

Sanam walks in and sits next to me, and as soon as she does, Mr. Lee claps to get everyone's attention. "Chess camp is two weeks away, and as you know, Katerina Nino will be joining us for the first day. She'll meet one-on-one with advanced players in the morning, and then host a training session for the rest of the team before she has to take off. To be clear, at this point I have not decided who will be selected, so work hard over the next two weeks and you might very well get picked." Sanam grabs my hand and squeezes. I squeeze back. "I've known Katerina for a long time, and she loves meeting young people who are excited about chess."

Even though all I want to do is jump up and down and scream, because I can't believe there's a chance I could be in the top twelve, I don't let myself do that. I close my eyes and take a deep breath. Right now, I need to focus so I can win.

And that's exactly what I do.

The rest of the week goes by quickly. I win my game on Wednesday! The only problem is that I keep getting distracted and looking away from the board. It makes me realize something important: I can't concentrate if I'm in the middle of a table. No chance. Even if my hyper focus and medicine are both in full effect, other people's breathing and sighing still really bother me. I have to be at the end of the table to play my best.

The next time Mr. Lee picks me to compete in a tournament, I'm going to tell him what I need to win. It seems like the kind of accommodation I should be allowed to have because of my ADHD, like how I can go to the learning center during tests and quizzes. I guess I'm just a person who needs things to be quiet if I'm trying to pay attention. I'm really glad I figured out what helps, because even though it doesn't seem like a big deal, I know it can make a huge difference.

Another good thing that happened this week was that I had an appointment with Dr. Gold. I told her she was right about medication. It makes my ADHD feel a lot smaller. She was happy to hear that everything has been better for me, even if things got a little worse at first. Also, I got a B on my math quiz and an A- on my lab report (high-five, Sanam—best partners ever)! By the tournament, it really feels like I'm turning things around.

Our team is playing at a middle school a few towns over. On the ride, Henley comes up with a cheer and makes Mom and Dad sing it to me: "Clea is the chess queen. That's what makes her opponents turn green. She's always on the winning team! Check. Checkmate. Win!" It doesn't matter that I'm probably not playing today, I'm still excited my family is coming to cheer for us, and I'm proud of how well I did in practice this week. I gave every game my all. It felt good to play like that again and I know if I keep working hard, I'll get a chance to compete in another tournament.

By the time I find our team room, everyone is already in a huddle around Mr. Lee. Sanam is standing on the outside of the group as close to the door as possible, like she wanted to make sure I'd be able to find her immediately.

"I want you to get out there today and give every game your all," Mr. Lee says. He looks at his notebook. My heart speeds up. I need to stop freaking out for no reason. There's a zero percent chance I'm getting picked. "Let's go with Sanam, Ajay, Red, and Ella," he says. Sanam and I exchange smiles.

Even though I know the order doesn't matter, I still think it's cool that her name got called first. "Isaac, Lily, Pari." Mr. Lee pauses. There are five spots left. I'd bet on Dylan, Mateo, Quinn, Hunter, and Layla. "Mateo, Hunter, and Layla," Mr. Lee says. *Check. Check. Check.* "And finally—Clea and Dylan."

I don't realize he's called my name until Sanam puts her hand up to high-five me. "So if you crush it today, which you definitely will—"

"I'll be in the top twelve for camp!" I finish her sentence. I know it's true as soon as the words are out of my mouth. It's weird how something can feel so close and so far away at the exact same time. I take a deep breath. I know what I need to do to win. "BRB. I have to talk to Mr. Lee about where I'm sitting before I'm stuck between a heavy breather and some-one who is sniffling every four seconds."

"Good call," she says. "Fingers crossed."

I cross my fingers on both hands and walk over to Mr. Lee. I really hope I can convince him that this is important.

I clear my throat and stand up as tall as I can. "I didn't think I was going to play today, otherwise I would have talked to you about this earlier. But it's hard for me to focus with my ADHD and it would really help if I wasn't in the center of the room or in the middle of a table."

Mr. Lee looks at his watch. "Let me see if there's anything I can do. I'll be right back."

I stare at the door and remind myself to breathe for what feels like forever, until Mr. Lee finally reappears. *Please. Please. Please.* I really need this to win.

"You're all set. You'll be at the end of the table in the far corner of the room away from the door for all three rounds," Mr. Lee says. "And I'll make sure you have the appropriate accommodations moving forward, so you won't have to ask me next time."

"Thank you!" I say.

"No, thank you," he says. "It was very responsible of you to say something. I can see that you're not only dedicated to chess and the team, but to your own needs."

"Is that a good thing?" I ask, because I can't really tell.

"Not good—*excellent*," he says. "I picked you to represent our team because I think you can win today. But great chess players have to believe in themselves. And now I know you do. You wouldn't have stood up for yourself and asked for the things you need to play your best if you didn't think you could win."

I nod, sure Mr. Lee is right about that. "I know I can," I say, because it's true, and right now I feel like I can do anything.

"That's great to hear," Mr. Lee says.

I turn around and run over to Sanam. "Two thumbs up," I say.

"Yes!" She puts up her hand, and we high-five.

I'm ready.

I don't get distracted once during the first round, thanks to my awesome seat in the quiet corner of the room. The only problem is that we draw, which isn't that great for me. But the good news is that drawing is a billion times better than losing, and since I lost all three rounds at my last tourney, I'm already improving!

In the second game, my opponent is at the same level as me. It makes me realize I'm actually really good! In the end, I can't find a way to beat him and the round ends in another draw. *Boo.*

When I sit down for the third round, I'm nervous. I want to win more than anything and this is my last chance. Jane and I go back and forth. *Move. Let go. Tap. Write.*

I slide my queen over, putting her king in check. It looks like I'm so focused on winning that I don't realize the black queen is about to skewer me. But I do. It's a decoy. I'm a magician. *Look over here, while I do something distracting with my not-so-little pawns, before you realize what's about to happen to you. Mwah-ha-ha.*

273

Jane does exactly what I want her to—she captures my white queen with hers.

I move my pawn up and place it on the far end of the board, so I can promote it! *Poof.* I turn my pawn into a queen. In an instant, the black king is back in check. Now Jane doesn't have a choice or another move, other than to get her king out of danger, which means her queen is about to be captured by my newly promoted queen. She slides her king to the side, and as soon as she taps the clock, I skewer her queen with mine. *Bye-bye. Decoy executed perfectly, if I do say so myself.*

I stay focused, backing her king between my king and queen, until, "Checkmate." I won for the first time ever in a tournament!!! And it's even better than I imagined. It feels like a sugar rush and getting an A and the first day of summer vacation all put together. Only better, because I feel like I'm floating out of the room and down the hall. I can't stop smiling, because I did it. I'm the winner. It's my victory. And no matter what, no one can take it away from me.

I see Sanam standing at the other end of the long hall between the cafeteria and the music room, looking right at me with nervous, hopeful eyes, like she's been holding her breath, waiting for me to appear with good news. As soon as our eyes meet, we run over to each other. "I won!" I shout.

"We won!" she shrieks.

"OMG. Yes!" We hug and jump up and down in circles until I'm dizzy.

"Clea. Sanam." Someone yells for us from the team room, halting our BFF-for-life victory party. It's Dylan. "We're all waiting for you."

Sanam smiles at me with her eyes and then leads the way.

Once I'm standing next to him, Dylan puts his arm around my shoulder. It's soft and warm. Then he leans in and whispers, "You rocked." And out of nowhere, there are a million butterflies flapping their tiny wings inside my stomach.

The whole team and most of the families are already in the room.

"Great work, Clea. I knew you could do it!" Mr. Lee holds up his hand.

We high-five. "Thanks!"

Henley runs over and squeezes me tight. "Winner. Winner. Vegetarian chicken dinner! That's you." She points to me. "And you. And you. And you," she says in her loudest voice and points to each of the people on the team, like she doesn't care who hears her. It feels big and important, like a victory for Henley.

She grabs on to my hand. "Let's go!" she says, pulling me over to Mom and Dad.

Mom hugs me first. "You're amazing."

"We're so proud of you." Dad holds on tight, like he wants to make sure I know how much he means it.

After the tournament, the whole chess team goes to The Hideout to celebrate our big win. The plan is that Mom, Dad, and Henley are going to drop Sanam and me off downtown. And while we're hanging out with everyone, Sanam's parents are going to bring a bag of her stuff over to my house, because our parents met at the tournament and obviously really liked each other and now she's sleeping over tonight for the first time ever!

I'm standing in the hall by the bathroom, waiting for Sanam while my family goes to get our car, when Red walks up to me. "Can we, um, talk?"

I shrug. "I guess."

He clears his throat. "I'm sorry I said I didn't want to be friends anymore."

"Then why did you say it?" I ask, because even though I want everything to be fine again, it's not and I can't just pretend. Not this time.

"Because I was sick of my dad letting me down and then

saying sorry and expecting me to forgive him. And it kind of felt like you were doing that, too, but it wasn't the same, because you actually felt bad about hurting me. And you were kind of having a hard time. My dad . . . he's only saying sorry because he doesn't want me to be mad at him. But he doesn't really feel bad about anything he's done. He likes Colorado and Barf. I was mad at him and I took it out on you. I shouldn't have done that."

"And Dylan," I say.

Red nods. "I know. I was a jerk to him too."

"Pretty much," I say.

"I'm sorry. I apologized to Dylan earlier." Red taps his foot, like he's nervous. "I really want to be friends again. Is there any chance you can forgive me?"

I think about his question, because I get that he's sorry, but I want to tell him the truth. "I mean, I forgive you, but the thing is I'm never going to be perfect," I say. "I'm doing my best and I think it's pretty good. But if I only have a certain number of chances left and you're keeping score, we probably shouldn't be friends."

"Because you don't want friends who are waiting for you to mess up, so they can be like . . . *see, you did it again?*"

I nod. "I just don't think that's good for me."

"I won't do that ever again," he says. "I promise."

"Don't promise. Just try really hard not to."

"Okay," he says. "I will."

Red steps closer and hugs me. And I hug him back, holding on tight, because I really missed him.

"Finally!" Sanam squeals and then runs over and wraps her arms around both of us and it feels so good.

When Sanam and I get to the Hideout, I go straight up to the counter and order our hot chocolates—dark for me, milk for her.

Quinn is standing by the barista, waiting for her drink, when I walk over. "Just so you know, everyone is talking about how you cheated in that last round," she says.

"Really? Well, I didn't. But good try," I say. "BTW, it's too bad you didn't get picked to play. That must be really tough."

"You're a loser if you think winning one match in one tournament changes anything."

"It changes everything," I say. And by the way she looks at me, I can tell we both know it's true.

"Two hot chocolates," the barista announces.

I pick up my order and walk away.

After Sanam and I finish our drinks, she disappears with

Red. And I end up sitting alone in front of the fireplace. I keep looking around for Dylan, but he isn't anywhere to be found, so I stare at my phone and pretend like I'm texting someone, even though everyone I know and text with is here.

"Hey." Dylan appears next to me. "Can I talk to you? Like maybe alone?"

"Yeah," I say. "Where?"

He tilts his head toward the door, like he wants me to follow him outside.

I get up, and then we walk out the front door and into the cold. We turn the corner onto a quiet side street. Once we're alone, he stops walking and looks at me. I can tell he wants to say something, but he doesn't, not right away. I bite down on my lip, because I don't want to say anything stupid and ruin whatever might happen. I can see his hands shaking and for a second I think it might be because he's cold, since we both left our jackets inside, but then I realize he's nervous. Before I think it through and stop myself, I take a step toward him and slip my hand into his.

He wraps his fingers around mine and squeezes, like he doesn't want to let go. My stomach flips.

"Do you, um, want to go out with me?" Dylan asks.

"I mean, we don't have to go anywhere. Or we can. I just mean, do you want to be my girlfriend?"

"Yes," I say before he has a chance to say anything else or take back his question.

"Okay." He smiles. "Good."

I smile back at him. And then before I know it, his lips are on mine and we're kissing. It's soft and sweet and mint chocolate flavored, and I'm not sure what I'm supposed to do with my hands, so I leave them exactly where they are, because I never want the kissing to stop. I want to stay like this forever.

Sanam and I change into our pj's and pick out a movie. It turns out she isn't really into magic, but she loves superheroes, which is new for me, but I'm on board. I like the idea of having top secret powers. We sink into the big sofa with all the snacks we can carry, and I'm about to press *play* and start *Wonder Woman* when she whispers, "Red kissed me."

"No way!" I say. "Dylan kissed me. And asked me out."

"Shut up. Wait—do you think the boys planned it?"

"No chance," I say. "Actually I have no clue."

Sanam takes a Twizzler and wraps it around her finger. "It was my first kiss."

"Mine, too," I say.

"I think I was bad."

"You weren't."

"How do you know?" she asks.

"Because Red has never kissed anyone else, so as far as he knows, you're the best kisser on earth."

She smiles and then takes a bite of her licorice.

"Wait—now I'm kind of nervous I was bad," I say.

"We just need to google," she says, and starts typing into her phone. "Am I bad at kissing?" She pauses. "Okay—did you bump teeth? Or move your head all over the place? Or slobber?"

"No. And ew!"

She laughs.

I do, too.

She looks back at her phone. "Did the person you were kissing push away?"

"Definitely not." I shake my head.

"Me neither," she says. "And you didn't have dry lips or bad breath?"

"Nope!" I say.

"Then, we're totally good at kissing!" she says. "Go us!"

Sanam is the kind of friend who makes everything better, even things that are already good.

SEVENTEEN.

ON MONDAY MORNING, Mom, Dad, and I have our check-in with Dr. Gold.

Everything in her office is the same. It still smells like gingerbread, the fancy chessboard is on her desk like always, and she's wearing another one of her bright dresses. Only everything feels different, because I am.

"How's it going?" Dr. Gold asks as soon as we're all seated.

"A lot better. The plan is working. And you were right about telling my teachers what I need. It really helps. Oh, and one more thing: I played in my chess tournament and I won!" I can't stop the words from flying out of my mouth. I've been so excited to tell her all of my good news.

Dr. Gold smiles at me. "I'm glad to hear that you're feeling good and doing well, Clea. That's wonderful."

"We think so, too," Mom says.

Dad nods.

"The only problem is that I have a lot of big assignments due this week and a history test. I'm sort of worried that it's going to be hard for me to get everything done and play my best in chess."

"How are you going to handle the competing pressures?" Dr. Gold asks.

"I made a list of everything I need to do, and I'll go to the library at lunch, because that actually helps me a lot. But I think I have to ask Mr. Lee if I can sit out of practice on Tuesday so I have more time to study after school."

"Clea, you don't have to do that," Mom says.

"We can come up with another plan," Dad offers.

I love them both for listening to me and getting how important chess is, but I know what I need to do. I shake my head. "I'll have a much better chance of playing well in chess and getting a good grade on my test if I skip practice, than if I try to do everything when I already know I can't, at least not yet."

"Are you sure?" Mom asks.

"It's definitely not what I want to do, because there's a chance that if I miss chess, I won't be in the top twelve anymore, and being in the advanced group at camp is like the real deal. It means you're officially good. And I wish I didn't need extra time to study, but I do, so yeah," I say. "I am." Because deep down I know it's the right thing for me, even if I wish it were different.

"That's very mature," Dad says.

Dr. Gold nods. "I understand that this is a difficult decision, but you're making the smart, thoughtful choice to think ahead and balance your responsibilities. I'm impressed. And no matter what happens with camp, I think that Mr. Lee will be, too."

I nod, because I know that's definitely true.

When I get to school, I knock on Mr. Lee's classroom door. "Clea, come on in," he says. "How can I help you?"

I walk over and take a deep breath. His secret T-shirt says *Arcade Fire*, which I think is maybe a band, but I'm not sure. "I can't come to practice on Tuesday, because I need extra time this week for homework. And even though chess is the number one most important thing in my entire life, if I get a bad grade in school, I won't be able to play or go to camp, and I think taking a day off from practice is what I need."

Mr. Lee looks at me and nods, like he's really listening and thinking carefully about what to say next. He leans against his desk and crosses his arms. "Strong chess players need to think ahead about how to win. But they also need to anticipate how they might get tripped up along the way. That foresight differentiates good players from great players. And that's exactly what you're doing right now—planning out a strategy so you can do your best."

"So you think I could be great?" I ask.

"You already are," he says. "Keep up the good work. And thank you for letting me know in advance. That helps me a lot."

"I will! Thank you! I'm going to work really, really hard in practice," I say.

"I'm glad to hear it."

I do my best in practice on Monday and Wednesday and give both games my all, finishing the week with one draw and one win. I'm not sure it's enough to make the top twelve. I think that's going to depend a lot on how other people played, since right now I'm on the cusp of being advanced.

By the end the week, I get an A on my Spanish project, a few check pluses on different homework assignments, and a B on my big history test! I feel like my study system is finally working and getting better every day. It feels good to keep improving.

When Mom pulls up in front of school on Saturday morning for chess camp, I know that no matter what happens, I did the right thing for me.

I'm about to open the door and get out of the car when Mom takes my hand in hers and holds on tight. "No matter what happens in there today, I think you're good enough to be in the top twelve."

"Thanks, Mom." I wrap my arms around her.

She hugs me back. "I love you," she says.

"I love you, too," I say. Then I get out of the car and walk inside.

There's a lump in my throat and a pit in my stomach, like when I first started taking medicine. Only as soon as I see Sanam standing by the door waiting for me, they both disappear, because even if I don't make the advanced team, I know it will be okay.

"Tell me," I say as soon as I'm standing next to her. "Just get it over with already."

"You're kidding, right?" She looks confused. "I definitely didn't look at the list without you, because (A) um, no, I'd never do that, and (B) checking the list without you seemed like bad luck or something."

I smile, because she's totally right, and it feels good to have her on my side. "I'm scared," I say. "I really want to make it."

"I know. But if for some stupid reason you don't, promise you won't give up."

"Never," I say, because that's one thing I know for sure I won't do. Not now or ever. "Falling down and getting back up is sort of my thing."

She grins. "It's like your superpower."

I smile back, because it's true, and I like thinking about ADHD that way.

Sanam and I grab on to each other's hands and walk over to the list. I breathe and scan the names:

ADVANCED CHESS TEAM

1. RED LEVINE
2. SANAM NASIMI
3. DYLAN JOHNSON
4. ISAAC ANDREWS

5. AJAY PATEL
6. LILY MARINO
7. LAYLA SHAH
8. MATEO COHEN
9. QUINN MCCLARAN
10. PARI VERMA
11. CLEA ADAMS
12. HUNTER JONES

Sanam and I scream at the same time, then hug and jump up and down.

I did it! I made the top twelve! It's the best feeling I've ever had in my life, because even though it was hard to get here, I know that no matter what happens I can get here again and again and again. It's a secret power that's always with me now, making me stronger and better and smarter.

AUTHOR'S NOTE

When I was in first grade, my parents took me to see a child psychologist, after my teacher called to tell them I was aggressive, unruly, and emotional. She said I couldn't sit still, or wait my turn, and that I wouldn't pay attention or follow directions. The child psychologist determined that I was frustrated and acting out because I kept falling behind in school. She recommended that I see a tutor, and so I did, twice a week for three years. The tutor drilled into me that I was responsible for my behavior and that I needed to be in control. She taught me—not so kindly—to cope with my symptoms.

I did not know I had attention-deficit/hyperactivity disorder, also known as ADHD, when I was a growing up. I thought I was slow and lazy, a forgetful person who made a lot of careless mistakes. And I didn't want anyone to know I was struggling, so I created study systems. I drank coffee to help me focus. I spent every weekend, all weekend, studying. I worked harder and harder. I refused to fail, but I still did, and when that happened, I talked to my teachers and took responsibility. I blamed myself.

It wasn't until I was twenty-one, a college graduate who had majored in English, and should have minored in theater—only I forgot to hand in the paperwork—that my parents told me my much younger brother had been tested for and diagnosed with ADHD. I remember the way they told me—like they were relieved to have answers and a plan to support him. Like it was okay to need help. And in that moment I knew I needed help, too. Adulthood was different from school. There were new rules that I wasn't used to and couldn't remember. There were bills and deadlines and meetings where it was not appropriate to speak up, much less say everything I was thinking out loud.

One of the hardest moments for me was admitting that I'd been struggling for a long time and realizing that asking for help didn't make me weak—it made me strong and honest and brave.

I wrote this book because ADHD is complicated and challenging, not just for the person with ADHD, but for their family and friends, too.

ADHD is a neurodevelopmental disorder that affects

people of every age, gender, IQ, race, religion, and socio-economic background. While boys are three times more likely to have ADHD and tend to be identified sooner than girls, early diagnosis and intervention are important for all kids with ADHD. When left untreated, adults with ADHD are at higher risk for a variety of mental health challenges and the disorder can have a significant impact on their education, employment, and relationships.

While Clea is a fictional character, she represents a lot of real people. For story and timeline purposes, I took liberties with how long some things, such as testing and results, would take. There is no single test to diagnose ADHD, and there isn't one way to manage the symptoms, but there are lots of options and support. Listed here are a few resources where you can read more about ADHD:

CHADD, The National Resource on ADHD
www.chadd.org
American Psychiatric Association
www.psychiatry.org
American Psychological Association
www.apa.org

ACKNOWLEDGMENTS

Kate McKean, my amazing literary agent, thank you for believing in my books.

David Levithan, thank you for getting why this book mattered from the beginning and for giving me insightful, honest, and always smart feedback. You've taught me so much, first as my teacher and now as my editor. I feel very lucky to have your support. Big thanks to Maya Marlette for knowing everything about chess and for sharing all the answers with me.

Thank you to everyone at Scholastic for supporting this book: Ellie Berger, Lizette Serrano, Robin Hoffman, Milena Giunco, Elizabeth Parisi, Baily Crawford, Bill Franke, and Jackie Hornberger.

Corey Haydu, Amy Ewing, Jess Verdi, and Caela Carter—you are my writing rocks. Thank you for telling me this story was important over and over, and for getting why I needed you to keep saying it. Cheryl Klein, I will be forever grateful to you for believing in me and teaching me how to write a book in a way I could understand.

I'm lucky to have so many amazing friends who get and accept me. I love you. You know who you are.

Thank you to all of my teachers for your patience, especially Mrs. White, who taught me to ask for help and to forgive myself for my mistakes.

I am grateful to Dr. D. for treating my ADHD, for helping me to understand my mind, and for teaching me to manage my symptoms. Thank you to my friend Dr. Nina Shiffrin, who advised and guided me to the right information, and to Meghan Shann for being an educational resource. Thanks to Dr. Sharon Saline, Corey Greene, David Kraemer, Dr. Rodriguez, and Bianca Territo for your help.

Caroline, Henley's character is based on our sisterhood and the unwavering patience and kindness you've shown me since the day you were born. Thank you for always giving me another chance to try again, even when I didn't deserve your understanding. I am better because of you.

Adam, I don't know where or who I would be if you hadn't been diagnosed with ADHD. You saved me. I hope this book shows every kid like us that smart, capable people come in all different packages.

Papa, there are no words to describe how special you are

to me. Gammie, I wish you'd had a chance to read this book. I think you would have liked it. I'll make sure there is a copy in your library. I miss you.

Mom, I struggled so much, for so long, and yet somehow you found a way to make sure I loved books and school and learning. Thank you for filling my world with stories, for valuing my voice, and for doing everything in your power to help me find my way.

Dad, I've never been afraid to try or scared of hard work or ashamed to fall, because of you. You showed me that the smartest people—people like you—who go to the most important schools and accomplish big things and help others—work and fall and get back up and do it all over again.

Juliette, right now you are small and growing every day. You are a wonder—fierce and powerful and determined. And I am thankful that at least for today I can fix all of your problems, just by being your mother. That won't always be the case. But know that whatever challenges you face—no matter how big they are and no matter how overwhelming they feel—they will make you strong.

Andrew, I let you see all the holes and the problems and

the things I thought were wrong with me, and it turned out that everything I thought was bad—you thought was good and special. You changed the way I saw myself. Thank you for teaching me to believe. It is the greatest gift anyone has ever given me. I love you.

ABOUT THE AUTHOR

Alyson Gerber is the author of *Braced*. She is a graduate of The New School's MFA in Writing for Children and lives in Brooklyn, New York, with her husband and daughter. Visit her at alysongerber.com and find her everywhere else at @alysongerber.